INFINITE DARKNESS

INFINITE LIGHT

By
Margaret Doner

Authors Choice Press

New York Lincoln Shanghai

Infinite Darkness Infinite Light

Copyright © 2000, 2005 by Margaret Doner

Authors Choice Press
an imprint of iUniverse, Inc.

iUniverse books may be ordered through booksellers or by contacting:

iUniverse
2021 Pine Lake Road, Suite 100
Lincoln, NE 68512
www.iuniverse.com
1-800-Authors (1-800-288-4677)

Originally published by Vivishphere

I Have Known You Twice, p. 145-146 used with permission of the author, Dean Doner

ISBN-13: 978-0-595-34740-7
ISBN-10: 0-595-34740-1

Printed in the United States of America

Acknowledgments

I wish to thank all the many people who have supported and taught me along the way. Editor, publisher and friend, Peter Cooper, whose unwavering belief in me kept me on the path—without Peter this book would not exist. Roger Woolger, Ph.D., my mentor, whose pioneering work in past life regression therapy healed me, and brought me "home." Laura Shore, who first mentored my writing efforts and shared many of my past life regression journeys. Michele Muir for her photographic inspiration. My Tuesday writing group—Amy, Angela, Dru, Elaine, Jeanne-Marie, Karen and Liz, who have shared the writer's ups and downs with me. Michelle, my friend, who shares the journey of Spirit with me. Kalia, my older sister, who has encouraged and aided my writing endeavors with an open heart and brilliant mind. My mother, Lois; my father, Dean, who continues to guide me through his spirit; and my younger sister Lauren—I love you dearly. The too numerous to mention friends who have loved and encouraged me—especially Catherine Trott, whose belief in the power of Synchronicity brought me to Peter. And especially, Chris, the most wonderful husband who ever walked the Earth—may we share many more lifetimes of happiness.

For Jamie,
in a century lost

INFINITE DARKNESS

INFINITE LIGHT

Chapter One

S weat tickles my nose and a drop disappears into my plastic cup of cheap white wine. I blink the salty wetness from my eyelids, wipe my lashes with a napkin, and stare at the black streak of waterproof mascara left behind. A moist arm touches my bare skin as I glance up at the enormous yellow and white striped tent. A canvas heat trap. Ten bodies stand between me and the ice-cooled strawberries on the buffet table. Then only one—that of a large woman shoving grapes into her mouth. It will be awhile before that spot is vacant. This scene needs blocking. Frustrated, I turn away but am stopped by red-faced, cigar smoking Lester Barnes.

"Victoria, how was your summer?" he asks.

"Hot, but even the New York City subways weren't this bad."

"Directing?"

"Yes. An off-off Broadway play written by a friend." I smile and turn my body sideways to escape. I am stopped by a man too deep in conversation to notice the gentle shove I give his back.

"Off-off Broadway? Does that mean New Jersey these days?" he asks coyly, his thick, pale pink lips arcing upward into a sneer.

"See you later, Lester," I say with an insincere smile before disappearing behind a convenient wall of intervening flesh.

Are all universities this bad I wonder? Or is it just the small New England ones? I need more wine. The liquor table is thirty feet away and surrounded by members of the English Department.

"I don't agree," the booming voice of Christopher Sharpe reaches me. "It's like saying all Freud was interested in was penises." I lean to the right to see the head and shoulders of the man Sharpe is talking to. "You are so naïve, Dennis," Sharpe continues. "It's those nineteenth century writers you specialize in. God awful." Sharpe's long, yellowed fingers wrap around an unfiltered cigarette. He places it to his lips with deathly force, and bites his teeth into the tip. "They bore the crap out of me."

I'm near enough now to see Dennis shift uncomfortably from one leg to the other and pull at the collar of his button down shirt. I have a sudden urge to rescue him. I touch Sharpe on the shoulder.

"Hey, Christopher, how was your summer?" I ask while smiling at Dennis, hoping he will recognize my gesture.

"More interesting than this."

"Dennis, I've been looking for you everywhere. I need to show you something," I say to the surprised looking stranger. I grab his hand and lead him out from under the tent. Emerging from the canvas brings me back to reality and I realize I don't know what to do with him now that I've saved him.

"I hope you wanted rescuing," I say, an involuntary blush starting up my neck.

"Wanted is an understatement. But to be fair to Christopher, you now have to show me something."

He is scary handsome. Even under the suit coat I can tell he is broad-chested—one of my favorite attributes in a man. "I'm Victoria. Victoria Barkley. Theater."

"Lovely to meet you." He folds his arms, expectantly.

"Yes?"

"I'm waiting for you to show me something."

My blush, which had been receding, starts anew. His eyes seem to be measuring, practically x-raying me. I cast around helplessly. "Well, there's always—"

"Manon, by the way."

"Manon?"

He extends his hand, laughing. When I look at him dumbly he smiles. "My last name. Christopher already gave you my first."

"All right, Dennis Manon. Let me show you the fountain," I say gesturing toward the modern art mousetrap of abstract design that serves as an oasis to the hot and tired, but does little for the eyes. I pull off my sandals, sit with my feet in the cold, bubbling water and lift the coolness with my hands to splash my face. Dennis, a bit tentative, sits with his feet on the ground and back to the water.

"Oh, come on! What are they going to do?" I say, giving him a gentle jab in the ribs. "Deny you tenure for cooling off your toes?"

"Is it that obvious?" he asks.

"Yep." I gesture toward his feet. "Come on. Take the plunge."

I watch as he carefully unties the laces of his sturdy leather shoes, tears them off and rolls his socks down off his feet.

"Move over. These babies are free at last." He swings his body around, and splashes both feet into the fountain. He mimics a sizzling sound, then chuckles, shaking his head.

"What's so funny?"

"Just laughing at myself. At my last school I would never have done something like this. They were so uptight, they measured the toilet roll after...." He hunches his shoulders. "Sorry, that was a bit over the line."

"Don't worry about it," I laugh. "It's the same here. I went through it last year. This year..." I splash my feet in the water. "I'm a free spirit."

Dennis looks at me enviously. "You got tenure?"

"God, it feels good," I say, covering up a minor pique at the surprise in his voice. I have to balance the scale here, let him know I earned my status. "I'm not quite sure how I got to this sleepy hamlet, but here I am: a tenured professor at St. George College by way of a degree from Julliard, a Ph.D. from NYU, a book entitled *No More Second Acts*, as well as having directed lots of off-off Broadway plays." I bend over slightly and demurely scoop the water higher and higher up my calves, glad that I remembered to shave my legs this morning.

Dennis reaches down and splashes a handful of water on his face. He pulls his right arm out of the jacket, then his left. With a challenging smile he dips his hands into the water and fakes tossing it into my lap. When I flinch, he laughs, rubs his hair with his wet hands, then pushes himself up to standing. The water reaches the middle of his calves and soaks the pant legs of his suit. "Come on," he says. "Climb in. Are you afraid?"

I look around to see if anyone is watching us.

"Come on, Madam tenure." He grins at me and extends his hand. Tentatively I stand up, and look down at his large hand, clasping mine. The gold band on his left finger catches me by surprise and I look away.

"God, this feels great," he says, feigning a water ballet step.

Suddenly my heart and bare toes feel chilled and I pull my hand from his and step from the fountain.

"Victoria, come back. You've made me a free man."

I turn one last time to look at him, daring myself to stare directly into his eyes. Too much time passes, too much heavy, warm air presses down on top of my head. As though he feels it too, his jaw tenses. We both draw in a sharp breath from the buzzing air between us.

When I can move again, I grab my sandals and wave them at his face. "Bye, Dennis. I'm glad I... rescued you." I run away on the hot pavement leaving him standing, knee-deep in cold water.

Chapter Two

Gary moves gracefully between the cappuccino machine and cash register of the Café Bacchanal—the only place that serves espresso in Cornwall, Vermont. The café sits on Main Street, squeezed between a used bookstore and a Subway sandwich shop. Two years ago McDonalds tore down the rock 'n' roll club across the street and put up golden arches. Gary's café stubbornly remains as an expression of its quaint, eccentric owner. I watch his long, loose-limbed body as he juggles three different tasks; making change, dusting the white froth with cinnamon, and smiling cheerfully at the blonde co-ed who greets him with a familiar and slightly flirtatious hello.

I move past brass Turkish lamps and overflowing bookcases to flop in my favorite armchair, tucked in between a Buddha on my right and a Tolouse-Lautrec poster on my left. The black earth aroma of strong coffee thickens the air beneath the red and gold canopy adorning the espresso machine.

"Hey, boyfriend," I say as I sit down.

He steams a large cup of cappuccino and winks at me. "Hey, Vick." He is the only man I know that can wink with just the right amount of sex appeal. My left eye squints and I blow him a kiss to disguise my pathetic eye blink. We've only been dating a year and a half but he's made me forget all previous beaus.

I'm sitting in the "Victorian corner," named for its heavy ornate feel and velveteen chairs; no two pieces of furniture in the coffee shop match and each seating arrangement has a different personality. I've just finished the first day of classes and I'm tired but

elated. I treasure the temporary rush of young school child innocence that returns in me briefly every year about this time.

"How about a cappuccino? No, make it a mochaccino. I feel
decadent," I call to him as he signals in my direction to get my
order. Opening my briefcase I pull out my appointment book already covered in black ink. Gary arrives with the coffee and pulls
his chair close to mine.

"Put your feet up on my lap, and let me rub them for you," he
says.

"My God, Gary, you'll gross everyone out. You touch my feet
and then their food!"

"Your feet are cleaner than the money I give back in change.
They're… organic. You know?"

I stare at him. "You are kidding, right?"

He gives me an innocent look, then chuckles. "Don't worry,
I'll wash my hands when I'm done. Stick those puppies in my lap
and relax for a minute." He reaches down, grabs my foot and
slides off my leather sandal. I lean back and let him cater to me.

"You amaze me." This comes out mixed with a moan of pleasure.

"Little ol' me?"

"Yes. This place is a zoo, you've got all new waitresses—all
running around like crazy—and you want to rub my feet."

"Let's keep this in perspective. What's more important than
your tired toes?" His grin is bold as he lowers his head to place his
lips to my foot for a secret kiss.

"My feet are really fil…thy." A slow tickle of thin lightning
crawls up the inside of my thigh.

"Mmmm…"

Then suddenly, "Gary! Gary! Help, I screwed up really bad!"
A young waitress runs up to us and grabs his arm. "I'm sorry, but
I really need you!"

"Gotta' go. Dinner tonight?" he asks. "My place or yours?"

"No way I'm cooking. You can bring over some Chinese food
or a pizza. That's my best offer. I'm swamped already and I've
got to get some sleep."

"Chinese at 7. See you then." He kisses me nimbly on the mouth and goes to rescue the panicked waitress.

As I sip my mochaccino I watch him with admiration. He is attuned to the art of living in a way I definitely am not. I find that exotic. I find his looks exotic as well—especially the dark eyes with no definition between pupil and iris. His wavy black curls cascade into a thick ponytail that hangs down his back.

I brush thin blonde wisps of hair away from my face and put on my glasses to study my teaching plans more closely. I glance up at Gary once more and a smattering of residual electricity from his toe-kissing completes its journey upward. I jerk my attention back to the papers in front of me.

Suddenly I feel the table shake and glance up to see Dennis Manon sit himself in the wing-back chair across from me, a cup of coffee in his hands.

"Victoria. Mind if I join you?" he asks.

"Of course not." I continue quickly to cover my mild shock at seeing him here. "Does anyone ever answer yes to that question?"

"They do in my department."

"That bad?"

He grins. "Oh, you tenured professors. How quickly you forget. If the first few hours are any indication, everyone in the English Department hates each other. It's God-awful."

"How sad. We are more an institution of higher fear than higher learning. Afraid of cuts, afraid of not getting tenure, afraid of students accusing us of some God-awful thing." Safe ground. We both smile and relax. The smile brings down my defenses—makes me forget, momentarily, the effect those eyes had on me the other day—allows me the freedom to explore them further. Yellow and green flecks dot the surface of his eyeball like a lure on the water. Suddenly I'm hooked pupil to iris, like a trout on the line. A light brown wisp of hair falls across his forehead and bounces up and down as he speaks and gestures with his hands. His lips are thin and perfectly shaped as they form words I don't hear. What's he saying? Sounds attack my heart—words float away unheard. I feel certain that everyone in the restaurant must sense this energy pulling us together. Everyone, I realize suddenly, would include

Gary. This thought causes me to reawaken and glance around the restaurant to see if my feelings have been obvious.

"Victoria?" I hear Dennis say. "Vicky? What do you think?"

I've been caught. I clear my throat. "I agree." Risky reply, but I hear an echo of him saying something about how the tenure process ignores the teaching skills of professors. Apparently my answer is appropriate. Dennis nods and shifts in his chair. "It's getting late. I'd better go."

I look around for Gary as he comes rushing into the café from the kitchen. "I guess you're right. I'd better be going as well."

We rise simultaneously, our eyes locked. I turn only briefly to wave to Gary as we exit. He winks again at me and calls out, "See you tonight at 7." I smile back at him and, although all I've done is converse with a colleague, I feel slightly guilty.

I walk home slowly in the fading light. The oak tree in front of my house catches the last rays of sun and I notice its leaves have a touch of yellow, orange and brown at the tips. Only fifteen minutes from campus, my tiny stone and wood single-story is situated between a broken-up Victorian crammed with students on the right and a white colonial sorority house on its left.

"Hello, Victoria," Mrs. Thompson, the Pi Gamma Delta sorority girls' "mother," calls and waves as she sweeps away the two stray leaves that have fallen on her doorstep. She has gray hair pulled into a hard knot at the nape of her neck, and as far as I can tell wears only sensible shoes with thick soles and dark-colored stretch pants with print long-sleeved shirts no matter what the weather dictates.

"Hello, Mrs. Thompson. Everyone settled in over there?"

"Everyone's fine. I see your cat's been digging in our yard again." She points to a tiny bit of grass that looks like it might have been disturbed by an outside force.

"I don't think so, Mrs. Thompson. Cats don't dig much. Dogs dig, not cats."

"They dig when they finish their business."

I don't know what to say to this bit of information so I say nothing and walk up the path to my front door. My two cats, Antony and Cleopatra, greet me as I open the door. Antony runs outside and immediately pees on Mrs. Thompson's lawn. I duck inside to remain ignorant of any scratching motion he might be performing. Cleopatra rubs against my legs.

I put my briefcase down on the telephone table and notice the faculty directory there. I lift it up and flip through the pages. "Manon, Dennis. English. Room 232. Ext. 512," I tell Cleopatra. "Don't you wish there was more about him here?"

She doesn't answer. I pick her up and walk to the kitchen to open a can of cat food. I notice a white slip of paper under a refrigerator magnet and pull it out to read. "Do not be fooled by reality," it says. "It is the highest form of deception." I remember how Gary and I laughed when he cracked open his cookie and read that one.

Chapter Three

Dennis is turned around at the chalkboard when I enter his classroom. Actually, it's a small auditorium with about one hundred seats. With only eight thousand students at the college it's a large class. My classes are small and intimate, attended mostly by theater majors. A few minutes late, I slip myself quietly into a seat in the back row, and to my astonishment not a head turns in my direction, so enraptured do the students appear to be by their teacher. He turns from the chalkboard and continues his lecture.

This is the first time I've had the opportunity to unabashedly stare at him. For a few minutes I match my energy to his, sensing the rhythm of his movements and gestures with my own body. His hands move through the air like a lover following the curves of his desire, then punctuate his thoughts with a gesture firm and powerful. Seventy pairs of eyes follow him—like cats fixated by a jiggling string. No one yawns, or looks bored. In fact, at the moment, the pens and pencils are still. With his words, he is painting a picture of the nineteenth century for them.

"What was the world like when Jane Austen was alive and creating her works of fiction?" I hear him say, and then the room around him blurs. I shake my head to bring his words into focus, but I am somewhere else altogether.

In my mind's eye I see a delicate young woman standing in a drawing room in front of an ornately carved mahogany fireplace. The large gold-gilded mirror above it reflects the back of her head and shows her dark brown hair swept up in a tight twist. Her black lace-up shoes stand on red and blue oriental carpets. A maroon high-back chair and a small table covered with a lace doily and a crystal lamp sit across from her. Her left hand, placed lightly upon the mantelpiece, trembles slightly. The only noise in the room comes from her dress—a floor length, crisp green taffeta; it crinkles as her breath forces its way into her tightly corseted torso.

The gentleman across from her seems familiar. Although I can't see his face, I feel strongly that I know him. I watch, as though in a dream, as the man approaches the mantelpiece, drawing closer to the woman, causing her to tremble and her heart to beat harder and harder until she can barely contain it in her chest. It is at that moment that I become her. It is at that moment that our hearts join, pounding out the fear.

"I love you, Jean. I have loved you from the moment I first met you," says the man.

"It is wrong. You must leave now," she says.

"I have tried. I have failed. I would do anything to be with you alone, even for one day," he says. He draws closer until she can feel his impatient breath on her right cheek. "I would go to the gallows for one kiss."

Her eyes remain focused on the far wall, her body aware of his every move. She is caught and frozen in the waves of his desire. Gathering all her strength, she pulls away from him to stop the kiss; she cannot bring herself to leave the room although she knows she should.

"Give me a moment of time alone with you," he pleads. "Meet me in Kensington Garden. Tomorrow afternoon at 2:00. The Northeast Corner."

"Perhaps," she says with a coy glance.

I awaken with a start from this vision to see Dennis notice me in the back of the hall. His smile is sexual, seductive, as though we have become a secret club of only two members.

What a vivid imagination I have. Uneasiness settles upon me like a thick, reptilian skin I can't shed. For the next thirty minutes of the lecture I keep returning to the room with the fireplace, to the woman in the green taffeta dress. I blame this daydream on those horrid Victorians and their repressed sexuality.

Books drag across tabletops, bodies shift, and all the students seem to speak at once before I realize the class is over. As the room clears Dennis walks up the aisle toward me.

"You are a wonderful teacher," I say as he nears me. I feel awkward.

"Thank you," he replies. "Do you mind if I listen in on one of your classes sometime?"

"No, no. Not at all."

He sits in the chair next to me, reaches out his hand and touches the back of mine. His fingertips are warm and I realize suddenly how cold I am. He seems about to say something, but stops before the words leave his lips. He sighs and withdraws his hand from mine. I force a yawn in a poor attempt to hide the naked way he makes me feel.

"I guess I'm tired. Getting back into the swing of things." I stand up and wait for him to do the same so I can exit the aisle. He stands slowly, and for a moment the front of our bodies are a little bit too close.

I walk outside and am accosted by the brilliant sunshine. The Campus Green is dotted with students, many of them alone. The Student Union, on the far end of the Green, was torn down and rebuilt in the 70s after a fire. A cement box with windows, it stands in hideous contrast to the ivy-covered stone and brick structures surrounding it. St. George's was founded in 1875—about the same time as the woman in my vision. Only men would have walked the pathways at that time. Suddenly I feel very tired. A large maple, already half yellow, beckons and I sit at its base and rest my back on the rough trunk. I close my eyes and bring up the picture of the Victorian lovers.

I can see her again. Yes, she is beautiful. A beautiful smile. Petite. Dark hair, deep blue eyes. Very striking. He is vague. Slowly he comes into view. Light brown hair. A wavy mop on the top of his head. A stiff collar and waistcoat. I hear him implore her to meet him the next day in Kensington Gardens. I think I agreed to see him. Oh my God. I agreed to see him.

"Victoria, we have a faculty meeting." I open my eyes to see George Carlisle, Theater Department chairman, walk by. He points his finger in the direction of the Theater Arts building and scowls.

"Yes, George. I know." I had completely forgotten.

"Well, don't be late. We have a lot of business to get to."

"Right-o!" I plaster on a carefree smile and slowly shift my weight in order to stand up. Convinced I mean to follow him, George strides onward.

"What's her name I wonder?" Then shake my head. What am I talking about? Her name? Why the hell does she have a name? She's a figment of my imagination for Christ's sake. I brush myself off, straighten the crease in my slacks and smooth my hair. Last year at this time I would have been wearing a suit. Last year at this time I didn't have tenure. My top, a red jersey scoop neck, cut perhaps a little too low, accentuates my figure.

I'm the last one into the room. Everyone looks at me.

"Hey, Victoria." The Department secretary, Pam Witherspoon, is the only one to say Hello. Lester Barnes grunts and looks away. George Carlisle sits stone-faced waiting for me to have my seat. Leslie Cameron, a tiny woman with a huge voice lifts her hand in greeting. We are the two female professors in the department. She teaches Speech. I wave back and sit down. Across from me is a visiting professor I don't recognize.

"Victoria, since you missed the introduction the first time I gave it, I'd like you to meet Tom Banks. Tom comes to us from Boston University to take Craig's place while he's out on sabbatical," says George.

"Hello, Tom. Nice to meet you." I take a seat and nod to the others. There are nine of us in the department. Three Ph.D.'s in Theater and one in Speech, a Lighting Designer, a Costume Designer, a Dance teacher and a Set Designer. Pam the secretary makes nine.

"Last year the students voted on the plays and musicals they want to see done this year," says George. "Most of us disagree with the choices, but what's new about that?" The faculty titters appropriately. "*Hamlet* was voted upon, but with some dissension about how it should be performed. As I am sure you all recall they wanted to do it in a nudist colony, but couldn't figure out where they'd hide the weapons." A much larger titter greets him.

"I'm directing it, and although I'd like to see it done in a traditional manner, I'm willing to do whatever the students want. It's their play after all," I say.

"They're already doing *The Maids* with men taking women's roles for Christ's sake! I'm not going to allow them to mess with *Hamlet*," George says.

Tom Banks smiles knowingly across the table at me. I smile back. I judge him to be in his forties. He's slightly balding with a gray mustache and wire-rimmed glasses. I look for a wedding ring and don't see one. He's probably gay.

"I don't want to direct it. I can't stand the thought of fending off irate parents who think that men performing in women's clothing is the Devil's playground. It doesn't seem to matter to them that in Shakespeare's day every part was played by a man," George says.

"I'm doing *Hamlet*," I say again.

"Anybody want to direct *The Maids*?" George asks.

"I'll take it on," says Tom. Everyone turns to look at him. I guess they are also wondering if he's gay.

"I'd be happy to give you any help you need," I say.

"And I'd be happy to assist you on *Hamlet*," he counters.

"Then it's settled, thank God. I don't have to direct a play this year, just the entire department." George looks pleased. "I have to get this out of the way." He lifts up a memo from the President's office. "Basically it says, 'No fucking around with the students.'"

We're slightly shocked by his use of the F word.

"I'm not naïve. Everyone knows my own wife was once a graduate student here. And Leslie is currently engaged to be married to a graduate student. But please, people, be discreet." He glares at Nick Tarkington. "Especially with the undergraduates." Rumor has it Nick impregnated a freshman last year, though to his credit, the same rumor had him paying for the abortion with his Mastercard.

I glance impatiently at my watch. Tom catches me and smiles again. I blush this time, feeling like a naughty child.

I close my eyes and immediately I can see her once more. A vision of the green taffeta dress starts my heart racing. I pop my eyelids open and see Tom, still looking at me. This time I look away.

Chapter Four

My psychotherapist, Dr. Ted Robinson, is waiting for me to speak. I'm not sure what to say, or that I want to tell him. Instead of a reply I scan the room, trying to gain comfort from the familiar sight of the sofa, the brass planter, and the box of tissues on the coffee table in front of me. Ted's rumpled sweater, corduroy slacks and hushpuppies usually put me at ease, but not today. I take a deep breath. "I had this vision."

Ted raises his bushy eyebrows. I suspect he likes visions. They are like dreams, with an extra touch of madness. "What of?"

"Well, I was sitting in on a class on nineteenth century writers, and suddenly in my mind's eye, I saw a woman, a Victorian woman, standing in a drawing room by a fireplace. There was a man in the room with her. He wanted to kiss her, but she was resistant. It felt illicit, dangerous, and very immediate. I can't shake the image."

Ted shifts in his seat but doesn't say anything.

"I can't really explain clearly. I've never experienced anything like it before. It wasn't a normal daydream. I mean I was watching this scene, but I really felt like the Victorian woman was me. I felt her emotions quite clearly. I know it sounds crazy." I lift my eyes and look at him for reassurance.

"I see," he replies in that chin-scratching psychoanalytic way. "What did the Victorian woman feel like?"

"She was trembling. Although I sensed she was deeply attracted to the man in front of her, I also sensed that she couldn't express her feelings for him. Perhaps she was married to someone else. I'm not sure. She was definitely ill at ease."

Ted is silent for a moment. He runs his hands through his gray-
ing mane of hair and strokes his neatly trimmed beard. It is enough
time to leave me feeling foolish and vulnerable. I grab a tissue out
of the box even though there are no tears to be wiped away. I
blow a dry nose to fill the space with sound.

Ted clears his throat. "Victoria, when you can't deal with real
life pressures you have a tendency to escape into a fantasy world.
We've been over this before."

I blush. "I know. But that was the tenure thing. It left me drained.
This isn't the same thing."

"There is always a psychological basis. You said you were in a
class on nineteenth century writers. Why were you there?"

"Just seeing how a new professor was doing."

"A new male professor?"

"Well, yes. Not that it's germane."

"Not germane." He studies me over his pad of paper. "You
don't think that you are somehow transferring your feeling inap-
propriately?"

I look down and play with the tissue between my fingers, twist-
ing it into a long, tightly woven strand. My throat is dry, and a
raspy, nervous cough escapes. "But the woman and the man seem
so familiar to me. I'm not explaining it well."

"How are things with Gary?"

"What does that have to do with anything?"

"Maybe nothing."

"Things with Gary are fine."

"Well then, are you nervous about teaching?"

"No. I'm not."

His eyebrows do that up thing.

I want to slug him. "What are you doing? Rooting around trying to find something that indicates I've gone crazy?"

He frowns.

"I'm not crazy."

He blinks.

I lie back on the sofa and close my eyes. I've done this before—been silent to see who breaks first. So far he has always
won. After five minutes I relax. He's not going to push me, I think.

Suddenly, I know it. Jean, her name is Jean. I see her again, standing in the green tafetta dress, fingertips resting upon the mantelpiece. She is so frightened. She feels so alone.

"Until you are ready to look at the underlying issues here I can't help you."

I open my eyes and turn my head. Ted is staring at me.

"What underlying issues? That I see things? That I'm being visited by the ghost of a Victorian woman?"

"Is that what you think?"

"For God's sake, Ted, I don't know what to think."

"I think you've got some work to do on your relationship with Gary."

"Well, maybe I do. But I don't see how the two are connected."

"Go home, Victoria. Make the connection and come back next week. Our time is up."

Leaving Ted's my mind is foggy, and I wander until I find myself standing on the steps of the University library. The pink glow of the evening sun illuminates the imposing iron and glass entryway. I pull on the heavy door, and sense its resistance to my weak hand. I use my body to brace it open, and walk into the cavernous entrance. Automatically I seek out a quiet corner on the uppermost floor. I sit on a stiff-backed sofa and close my eyes. I'm in the drawing room again. Jean stands near the mantelpiece, her suitor before her. Again he walks over to her and she pulls away to avoid the kiss. Again he begs her to meet him in Kensington Garden. She turns to leave the room, but this time he walks boldly over to her and grabs her hand and presses it to his lips. She does not tear it away, but closes her eyes and lets her fingers linger on his lips, savoring the softness of his touch. When her eyes open, she sees his, staring at her. Quickly she pulls her hand away and turns to exit the room. In her haste, she knocks a crystal vase onto the floor....

BANG!

I jump. My eyes open. I have the look of a trout reeled in and gasping for air.

Dennis Manon wheels around, apologizing for the book he dropped onto the library floor. I look up into his face, but I see the

Victorian lover, and all I know is that I feel so strongly for him at this moment that I reach my hand in his direction and pull him down on the couch beside me in a gesture of pure instinct. My startled face stares into his startled eyes.

"Dennis," I whisper.

"Victoria? Are you all right?" Dennis holds my hands. He must sense my need to cling to him. I bow my head.

"I've seen something," I say. My hands tremble as Jean's trembled with the touch of her lover.

"You've seen something?"

I reach out my hand and touch his face and for a moment it seems so natural.

He looks down at his own legs. "You know I'm married. I have a child."

I draw away. "I know."

"I didn't mean—" he says, but I interrupt him.

"I know you didn't." If he had taken a knife from his pocket and stripped the skin off my body bit-by-bit at that very moment he couldn't have left me feeling more naked. The floor rises up to meet my gaze. I notice each speck of dirt that lies encrusted in the carpet. My cheeks redden and my throat clogs with saliva.

Dennis shakes his head as though to dispel the temporary fog that has engulfed him too. Neither of us has an explanation for what transpired, nor do we know what words to say. Still dazed he stands up and looks down at me. Briefly he touches my cheek with his fingertips and then turns and walks away in silence.

Chapter Five

I t's the time of day I like most in Gary's café. Between 4-5, the hour before closing, it clears out until he locks the door and it's just the two of us. I love to relax at the end of a day of teaching by sitting back and sketching the students, so I keep a drawing pad and some charcoal and pastels behind the counter. Occasionally Gary puts one of my sketches up on the wall with a thumbtack. If a student recognizes him or herself they don't object; I can tell they feel slightly honored at being singled out.

I've always loved the feel of charcoal in my hands. The way it blackens my fingertips with its soft dust. The longer I work the further the blackness travels up my arms, until some days I look like a coal miner from the elbows down. Today, instead of relaxing by leaning back in the padded chair and scanning the room for my next subject, my shoulders are tense and I stare intently at the paper, letting my gaze travel inward. I am searching my unconscious for any trace of Jean and her lover that are housed there.

The first sketch, of her against the mantelpiece, reminds me how clearly I do see her. How I know what it feels like to be enveloped in her skin, trembling and fragile. How heavy the material of her dress is, and how tightly her corset hugs her ribcage. When I've finished I glance up and see the room is empty. Gary is busy at the cash register and we are alone. I lean back and close my eyes, hungry to enter Jean's world once again.

Where does she go? Do they meet in Kensington Gardens? An image of a white parasol, with green lace trim, comes to me. The dress is also white and green, with large bows up the front and a green velvet ribbon about the throat. Her shoes are light colored today, laced up the front with pointed toes and a heel. She walks quickly, she hadn't dared to take the carriage, afraid the driver would question where she was going and why.

... Jean sits on a bench in Kensington Gardens trying to act nonchalant. Women of her class never sit alone in a public garden. It is a warm day and the parasol in her left hand keeps the sun out of her eyes and face but does little to relieve the mid-day heat. Her right hand flutters a fan nervously back and forth, far too rapidly for optimal effect. Her eyes scan the horizon, searching out a familiar face.

Maybe he won't come. Then won't I be the foolish one for agreeing to meet this love-sick man? She can almost convince herself that the whole thing never really happened, or at least that she had misconstrued his intentions and perhaps they were meant honorably—a momentary outburst and nothing more. "After all, he is my husband's good friend. My husband has taken it upon himself to assist him in many ways. He owes my husband a great deal."

Her searching eyes stop upon his form. He is tall and well dressed in a light gray suit and matching waistcoat. His body has the easy confidence of a man in his early twenties—strong and assured. The only indication of his feelings is in his pace: he is walking too fast. He will draw attention to himself. She pulls the parasol closer around her face and quickens the beat of the fan.

"Jean, thank God you've come," he says as he sits down right next to her.

"Mr. Ebcott," she begins, maintaining her focus outward, away from him.

"Franklin. Call me Franklin," he interrupts her with a broad smile and touches her hand. His earnest brown eyes search her face for feelings.

"Mr. Ebcott." She forces herself to look boldly into his smiling face and confront the unbridled, childlike passion held there. His face tells her more than she can bear: it says that her love alone can make his world complete. "It is daylight, or have you forgotten that I am a married woman and that my husband is your good friend?"

"I have forgotten none of this, but it no longer matters to me." He looks into her eyes. Her lips tighten, but they can do nothing to deter him. "My love for you is a sickness. A sickness for which there seems to be no cure except to have you in my arms. I had no idea that such love could exist until I met you."

"If anyone knew I was here...." she says.

"But they do not?" He looks for reassurance and speaks quickly, fearful that she will rise up and leave him with his unfulfilled longing.

"No, they do not." She turns away and stands, eager to put some space between them. Anything to gain strength. She walks away and leans against a tree, her back to him. She doesn't notice that he reaches out his hand to touch her and withdraws it before making contact. She cannot see the helpless look in his eyes.

His voice is strained. "I have no other recourse but to be totally honest with you, Jean. I am hopelessly in love with you. I have loved you from the moment I saw you."

"Franklin, what you propose is immoral. I am not a free woman. My wishes in this matter are of no importance." Her voice steels against him.

He places a hand on her shoulder and wheels her around. "You are a free woman. He does not own you as though you were a slave. And you love me. Can you honestly tell me that you would be here today if this were not so?"

The force of his gesture startles her and she draws on her remaining strength to fight him. "I will not be talked to in this manner!"

There is anger in his reply. "You do not love him, I see it in your eyes. You are in love with me. Your eyes do nothing to discourage my advances."

She knows he is right. The moment she agreed to meet with him she gave herself away. The thought terrifies her and she yells at him fiercely, "Leave me alone! What does it matter that I tremble when you touch me? Can it really change anything that you make me weak and confused and I long to kiss you as well? If you love me, you will leave me alone and end my suffering. Please. Go!"

"I cannot. Now that I know how you feel." Franklin grabs her and kisses her: In the middle of the park, another man's wife, in daylight for all to see. For the few moments his lips are upon hers, she cares for nothing but the man who owns them; any concerns about her reputation are washed away by the strength of the passion he awakens in her....

"Victoria?"

I open my eyes to see Gary's father, Herman, plodding heavy-footed and humpbacked out from behind the swinging kitchen doors. An unlit pipe is clenched between his teeth. Most of his hair is gone, and his nose has become even more prominent in old age. He leans over me; he has the sweet, rich smell of pipe tobacco.

"Did you fall asleep?"

"I don't know."

He smiles at me and extends his hands in a surprisingly gentle and sensitive touch to my shoulder. Although his features are harsh and his manner gruff, his eyes are kind and deep beneath the heavy eyebrows. He looks down at the picture on my lap. "What's that?"

"I'm just sketching."

"It looks old-fashioned... like the nineteenth century."

"I guess it is. Something that came into my mind, that's all."

He lifts it up and walks to the front window to look at it more closely. "It's good. What's the inspiration?"

"I don't know. Just came to me."

"Ready to go?" Gary asks.

I look confused.

"I'm taking you kids out to dinner. Lotte has gone to visit her sister and I'm all alone," says Herman.

"Oh, that's right. I'd forgotten. Let me grab my stuff." I pick up my briefcase and for a moment I realize I'm searching around the perimeter of the chair for my parasol. I take the sketchpad from Herman, put it under my arm and signal I'm ready to leave.

"Aren't you going to leave that here?" Gary points to the drawing pad.

"I think I'll take it home tonight."

Gary places his hand on the small of my back and we walk out the door. "The town is talking about okaying the plans for a Dunkin' Donuts to open across the street. Next to McDonalds."

"You're kidding," I say.

"I wish I was. Do you think in twenty years that every mid-size town in America will look exactly the same? McDonalds next to Dunkin' Donuts next to The Gap next to Kinkos?"

"Are you afraid you'll lose business?"

"The students don't want to sit in Dunkin' Donuts next to the cops," Gary says.

"You're right," I agree.

"Now if a Starbucks opens then I might be in trouble."

"What's Starbucks?" Herman asks.

I never cease to be amazed at how separate Herman manages to keep himself from the world.

"It's a coffee shop, Dad."

"Why would somebody open a coffee shop next to another coffee shop?" Herman asks.

"You're better than Starbucks," I say.

"Gee honey, now I know how you really feel." Gary kisses me on the forehead and laughs.

When we walk into Micheletti's, the local Italian restaurant, I see Mrs. Thompson seated with a male friend near the window. She is wearing her usual flowered shirt and black stretch pants, he has slicked-back black hair, a round boyish face and is wearing a bolo tie. Instead of a horse's head or a piece of turquoise holding the strings together, I notice what appears to be Jesus on the cross.

"Hi, Mrs. Thompson," I say loudly as we take our seat across the room. "I wonder if that's her boyfriend?" I whisper to Gary.

Mrs. Thompson gives me a half-hearted smile and turns away.

"She doesn't like me," says Gary. "I've got long hair, I run that disgusting student hangout and to top it all off I'm Jewish."

"Worse than that—you're a Jewish-Buddhist," I add.

"The greatest sinner in all of Cornwall, Vermont."

"And that makes me your Jezebel."

"What are you talking about, a Jewish-Buddhist?" asks Herman. "What the hell is a Jewish-Buddhist? You got another mother I don't know about? One with slanted eyes and straight black hair?"

"It's nothing, Dad."

Herman grumbles and picks up the menu. "Jewish-Buddhist," he mutters.

The waitress arrives to take our orders. She has pink and green hair, and the gold bead in her cheek makes me wince. I'm afraid to look in her mouth. "I'll have the spaghetti with pesto and vinaigrette on my salad," I say. "And a glass of red wine. House wine is fine."

"Make that two," says Gary.

"That was easy," says the waitress.

"You got some kind of veal parmigiana?" asks Herman.

"Dad, you shouldn't eat veal," says Gary. "It's awful what they do to the baby cows."

"Yeah, we got veal parmigiana," says the waitress.

"Give me one of those," says Herman.

"What do you want on your salad?" asks the waitress.

"You got blue cheese?"

"Yeah."

"Give me one of those." Herman reaches across the table and hands her the menu.

"Cool," says the waitress as she glances at his exposed arm. "You got a tattoo. I got one too, but I can't show it to you. It's on my butt. How come you got numbers? I never saw anyone get numbers before. What, you an accountant or something?"

My heart stops. I look at Gary; the color has already drained from his face. For a moment nobody speaks.

"I didn't have a choice," says Herman.

"Got drunk, huh?" says the waitress as she picks up the menus and walks away.

"Look at her; pins in her face, tattoos on her butt. Kids these days don't know what suffering is, so they have to invent it. For them it's a luxury. God! Imagine growing up so privileged you have to pretend at suffering." Herman shakes his head and scowls at me.

"I never thought of it that way. But, you are absolutely right," I reply.

Herman looks away from me. He doesn't want me to sympathize. He looks at Gary.

"She's just a kid, Dad. You know how teenagers are."

"Not in my day. We understood something of the world."

"Dad, you can't compare."

"She should suffer like I did." Herman looks at me. "All of you should suffer like I did. Then you'd appreciate what you have."

Chapter Six

The next morning I'm lying alone in my queen-sized brass bed. Herman was sullen the rest of the evening and by the time we went home Gary and I felt bullied enough by his anger that we both decided silently that it would be best if we went to our separate homes rather than risk appearing like "immoral youth."

Herman is wrong about one thing; some of us try to avoid suffering, even pretend acts of suffering. I have designed this piece of my world to eliminate suffering. I draw the white down comforter up around my neck and smile. A violet, green and yellow patchwork Amish quilt hangs on the wall opposite me, next to an antique dressing table. Antique perfume bottles catch the morning sun from their perch by the window. Blue, green, rose, purple, red, simple, elegant; I've collected them for years. A three-foot high tinkling Zen fountain—a present from Gary—sits in the corner nearest the bed. Water cascades gently down a slab of slate and lands on shiny, smooth black stones at the base. Antony curls up at the end of the bed and observes me coolly; his long gray striped tail flicks back and forth as his green eyes stare at me. Cleopatra purrs loudly and lies at the crown of my head. Occasionally she licks my hair, cleaning it as she would her own, then puts her creamy white paw across my forehead.

I roll over lazily and stretch. A fragment of last night's dream hovers. One image sticks in my mind. I remember a girl standing on a hill in the rolling countryside. Green fields stretch out around her. In a valley below her is a plow; the old-fashioned kind, shaped like a V and drawn by horses.

I reach for the sketchpad next to the bed. I'm glad I brought it home. My brows knit, concentrating. The girl has a long brown skirt with a white apron on top of it—like a peasant girl. There is a small cottage behind her and a path leads to the cottage.

I'm sketching madly now as the images come more clearly. Cleopatra jumps off as I sit all the way up in bed and tuck another pillow behind me to brace my back. The woman is putting out some clothes to dry in the warm sun. She is young, maybe seventeen. I draw her body; it's small and delicate and her dark brown hair, thick and luxurious, is tied back into a ponytail. She is thinking about something, I realize. She is deep in thought. The curves of her body as she hangs a man's coarse shirt over a line match Jean's curves. But where Jean's body was rigid and upright this woman is freer, not confined by a corset or high collar.

… As she hangs clothes out to dry in the warm sun the sound of a horse approaching draws her attention. "It's him. Mr. Cobb!" She runs a hand through her hair to neaten it as his carriage stops and he steps from it and walks toward the cottage.

"Mr. Cobb. Hello." She waves timidly from behind the wash. He is elegantly dressed, wearing a crisp, starched shirt, collar and elegant waistcoat. She notices a pocket watch chain hanging across his chest.

"Why, Jean, I was hoping I would see you again. You are actually the reason I stopped by."

Never has a man been so forward with her. Jean looks down at her feet. She finds it difficult to relate to this city man. She realizes that she does not know the proper manner in which to address him. Should she appear bold as she imagines the fine, sophisticated women he is used to must be? Or should she remain distant and formal, acknowledging their class difference?

"My father is out, Mr. Cobb."

Mr. Cobb walks toward her. He pushes aside the laundry and takes her hand. "Then take a walk with me while we wait for him to return."

To draw her hand away would be rude. "The washing. I've so much to do."

"Upon your return. Come. A walk in the sunshine will do you good."

"If you insist." She steps around the washing and allows herself to be led down the path, away from the house.

For a couple of minutes there is an awkward silence. Finally Mr. Cobb speaks, "You must have many suitors."

"None that are of any interest to me."

"None? That is difficult to believe. Tell me then, what does interest you?"

"You will laugh."

"Never." He crosses his heart with his hand and looks into her eyes. "You can trust me. I would never laugh at the dreams of a lady."

It is at that moment that Jean really sees the man. Beneath the dark wisps of hair that brush his forehead, she notices his eyes are a deep blue. They are kind and generous eyes, and she detects a sense of amusement just below the surface. His thin mouth is creased with smile lines, and by the slight gray at the temples, she judges him to be near forty, much older than she is, but still handsome and certainly quite solid. She is surprised to notice some attraction on her part. She draws herself up full height to meet his challenge. "Books. Books and writing are my interests. My father and brother tell me these are not worthy pursuits. I am told a woman needs a man, not an education." She lifts her chin with a haughty pride. She is accustomed to having to defend her beliefs to those around her.

He stares at her in far too earnest a manner. What could he possibly find of interest in me, she wonders?

As though reading her thoughts he answers, "Not only are you beautiful, you are also intelligent and well-read. It adds to your beauty. Your eyes, they shine. This is rare. Knowledge is never wasted on a man nor on a woman."

Jean has never met such understanding when speaking of her desires. "My father would disagree."

Mr. Cobb smiles at her and brazenly reaches out his hand to rest it on her shoulder. "I see. I hope this does not mean you do not like the company of a man."

"Oh, no. Only that a woman needs more."

"Perhaps that is because you have never been in love."

Jean understands his meaning. She blushes from the suggestion of his words and it takes her a moment to reply. She knows he is right. She has never been in love, nor has she had the slightest intention of marrying any of the men from her village. She also knows that without marriage her life will be difficult at best. "Perhaps not," she replies and smiles at him coyly. . . .

Five sheets of drawing paper are laid out on the bed. I barely remember doing the work. I stare at them. In the first picture Jean is hanging out clothes. Then comes Mr. Cobb alighting from the carriage. In the third he takes her hand and they step onto the path. In the fourth they are walking and talking. In the fifth he kisses her hand.

This man, this Mr. Cobb, is not the same man that approached me in the drawing room. If this is Jean then what is she doing here? And who is this Mr. Cobb? Mr. Cobb does not make me tremble in the same manner as Franklin.

I put my head in my hands. Cleopatra jumps onto the bed and crumples the fifth picture. "Get off, Cleopatra, you'll rip it!" I lift her off the bed and glance at the clock. It's eleven o'clock already. Holy Shit! I'm supposed to be at a meeting for *The Maids*. I told Tom I'd help him. "Damn!" I jump out of bed in a frenzy and knock my right knee on the nightstand. "Ouch! Damn it!" I hobble to the bathroom and turn on the shower. "I'm going to be late. Shit!"

Tom Banks's office door still says *Craig Bosley* on it—the name of the professor he is replacing. I tap lightly and push it open. Lester Barnes, the lighting designer, Nick Tarkington, the set designer, and Karen Low, the costumer, all turn around in their chairs and stare at me. Tom is leaning back on a wooden chair with his feet up on the desk. He is facing the door and he lifts his hand in greeting as I enter. "Welcome," he says.

"You're late," says Lester, stating the obvious like a first grade teacher to a naughty pupil. God, how I want to stick my tongue out at him.

"Sorry." The only available chair is a metal one, folded up and leaning against the built-in bookshelves. The room seems identical to the way Craig left it. There are too many books for the available shelf space and African masks and musical instruments are hanging on the walls or piled up in the corners. I pull up the chair and unfold it next to Tom.

"We were just discussing how to handle the irate parents and community members who, without a doubt, will accuse us of trying to encourage homosexuality. I'm committed to doing it with men in the roles of the women," says Tom. "Besides, art is supposed to infuriate people. It's the job of artists to push buttons and stretch boundaries."

"Does that mean I should let the kids do *Hamlet* in the nude?" I ask.

"There's no artistic reason for them to do it in the nude," says Tom.

"Hey, they're twenty years old, they want to show off their bodies. What other reason do they need?" adds Karen. Karen is about one hundred pounds overweight, and I detect a note of envy in her voice.

"I think Tom is right. Fuck 'em," says Nick. He rolls up the sleeves of his flannel shirt, as though he's ready to get to work immediately. I notice his hands are thick and callused from years of pounding nails and hauling wood.

"My job is to realize the playwright's vision to the best of my ability. In my opinion Genet's choice to put men in women's roles was not driven by his homosexuality. I think he was obsessed with the idea of the artificiality inherent in the theater. In order to achieve that he needed to have a man play a woman. Essentially he wants everything to be so false that it annoys us," says Tom. He looks from one to the other of us to see our reaction.

"It's a difficult show," I say. "We have three men playing the parts of women: two maids and Madame. The maids both hate and love their mistress. They try to murder Madame, fail, then one of them takes her own life. It's not a barrel of laughs, this play. I say let's forget the parents and get to work." I pause and look at Tom, then at Lester, but neither one speaks. "You'll love working with Barney, Tom. He is one of my favorite students, and an excellent actor."

"That's good to hear. Karen, do you have your sketches of the costumes?" Tom asks.

Karen unzips a large, black portfolio and withdraws about twenty pieces of paper from it. It suddenly occurs to me that she would be the perfect person to ask about the clothing that Jean was wearing in my vision.

"Karen, what was women's fashion like in the ninteenth century? Did it change dramatically from year to year, or stay relatively the same for decades at a time?" I ask.

"Sometimes the changes were year by year," she replies. "The crinoline-cage, like Scarlet O'Hara's, didn't come in until the late 1850s. By the end of the century women had gotten rid of the large skirts and were even wearing a type of tailored suit with a small bustle. But, of course, these were wealthy women. Peasants didn't have the money to afford the fashions of the day."

"Would you look at some sketches I'm doing?" I ask.

"Sure, I'd be glad too."

Lester glares at me. "I've got things to do today so could we get back on the subject?"

"Sorry, Lester." I look at Tom to see if he is angry. He's relaxed as ever.

"Madame has the most costumes, obviously. She's getting ready for a party. The other two stay in black," says Karen. "I've done a number of sketches. Different approaches and looks."

"The set is easy because it's one location. Madame's bedroom," says Nick. "Since Genet wrote it in prison and had nobody to change sets, I luck out. No set changes."

I'm staring at Karen's sketches. One of the sketches shows Madame with a man's face and neck protruding from a long, emerald green ballgown. It makes me uncomfortable, as if someone drew a mustache on my picture of Jean standing by the mantelpiece.

A few days later I walk to Ted's office scanning the streets for a glimpse of Dennis. I feel like he is avoiding me and it upsets me to think it is a possibility. I can't say I blame him if he is. But then, I think, how would he know to avoid me? How would he know where I am?

Besides, we haven't done anything wrong. He might think I'm a little weird for the scene in the library, but I'm probably just being paranoid. He probably doesn't even think about me at all. I probably think about him and he doesn't think about me. He probably doesn't even care whether or not he avoids me. I'm probably making this all up. He probably thinks I'm insane. I probably am insane. He is probably telling everyone I'm insane and laughing about me behind my back. Oh my God! Ted! Help!

"Victoria, come in." Ted opens the door for me.

"Ted. I had another vision." I don't even give myself time to sit down. "I want to understand what's happening here. Am I going nuts?"

"Sit down, Victoria." He indicates the sofa.

I sit stiff and upright. "Ted, I'm serious."

"What visions are you having?"

"Now she's a peasant girl. Standing in a field somewhere in the countryside. An older gentleman greets her and takes a walk with her. I woke up with it. I woke up from a dream with the picture of the girl in the field. Then I started sketching and a story unfolded in my mind. I can't really explain it."

"I think we should talk about you and Gary," he says.

"Me and Gary?"

"Yes, and anyone else that might be threatening that relationship."

"Threatening that relationship? Threatening that relationship?" I'm like an incredulous parrot.

"Yes. Have you met another man recently?"

"No."

"You sure?"

"Yes."

"I don't believe you."

That's the first time Ted has ever said those words to me. I can't believe he said them. I fold my arms across my chest like a belligerent child.

"Think, Victoria. Another man?"

"Well, there's Tom Banks."

"Who is he?"

"A visiting faculty member in the Theater Department. He seems very nice."

"Is he married?" asks Ted.

"I don't think so."

"Anyone else?"

"Well, there's Dennis, I guess."

"Dennis?"

"He's just an English professor. He was teaching the class I sat in on. You know, when I first saw Jean."

Ted raises his eyebrows at me. "Is he married?"

"Yes."

Ted raises his eyebrows again.

"What's that supposed to mean? Like I'm only attracted to married men?"

"You tell me."

"Gary's not married."

"No, but your last boyfriend was."

"I didn't know he was married," I protest.

"Doesn't matter."

"Doesn't matter? Of course it matters that I didn't know he was married when I slept with him."

"No it doesn't, Victoria."

"This is absurd, Ted. You want to talk patterns in my love life? What about Jewish men? I've had more than one Jewish lover. My first love was an Israeli named Amiele."

"Let's talk about you and Amiele then." Ted clears his throat and picks up his pen. I realize this is going to be new information. I haven't spoken about Amiele to anyone in years.

"I met him at a performing arts camp in upstate New York. He was tall, dark, handsome and by seventeen he had already learned how to please a woman; he told me it was intuitive. He loved women so much that he knew automatically what they liked. I wanted to believe him, so I did. He was a dancer: me, a wanna-be actress. Sent by my parents to this camp to find out how serious I was about a life in theater."

I stand up and walk over to the window. Remembering this time makes me feel young and vulnerable again. "He had soft, dark brown penetrating eyes and a passion for the theater that was contagious. I opened my pores and saturated myself with him. I surrendered everything I was to him, never imagining that perhaps it might be wiser to keep a little aside just in case I was left in the end with nothing. Forever was easy to say at sixteen."

I turn around to see Ted staring back at me. I suppose he's happy that this memory takes place during this lifetime. I come back to the sofa and sit down. "Every attendee of the camp had to have two theater experiences: backstage and onstage. The production of the summer was always a big musical. There were two casts and half the summer you would be onstage, the other half you would switch places and work backstage. I was onstage in the chorus the first half of the summer and backstage the second. Amiele was doing his onstage time in *Guys and Dolls* while I assisted the costumer. It was my job then to make sure everything was hung up and put away properly. It was around midnight after a performance when I remembered I hadn't hung up one of the lead actor's suits. I'd left it on the ground where he had flung it and it would surely be wrinkled and me to blame if I didn't go back. Reluctantly, I grabbed a flashlight and headed out of the bunkhouse. It was a full moon night. I remember being amazed at how bright everything was outside and how I almost didn't need the flashlight. Being a child of Manhattan I don't think I'd ever experienced being illuminated solely by the moon before. Anyway, you can probably guess what's coming."

"Amiele in the arms of another?"

"I wish."

"So?" asks Ted.

"Amiele with his face between another girl's thighs."

"Oh!"

"To a sixteen year old girl that's more sacred than intercourse. At least it was to me. I ran out of the theater and into the surrounding woods and sat down on a log and cried until a touch on my shoulder startled me back to reality."

"Amiele?"

"Nope. He was probably still using his intuition on the naked girl. This was a man I didn't recognize. He said he was a visiting director. I wasn't afraid of him. His manner was very gentle. He pulled out a clean hanky and handed it to me. I was very grateful for that hanky—when I finished blowing and sniffling he talked to me, but not about love or broken hearts or all the fish in the sea. He talked about theater and art. How it was the duty of an artist to tell the truth, to be fearless about living, to be bold and courageous and not to shy away from experiencing life in all its glorious extremes."

"This struck a chord in you, I take it." Ted has his arms folded, not taking notes.

"Yes." I feel a momentary embarrassment for my younger self, then shake it off. "He said the artist must hold up a mirror so that others can see themselves clearly in it. Joy, pain, anger, fear, betrayal, rapture, lust, greed, desire, there is no limit to the range an artist must be willing to explore. 'It is your duty,' he told me. Then he said, 'The hell-fire of life consumes only the best of men, the rest stand by warming their hands.'"

"Your 'visiting director' was quoting Fredrich Hebbel."

I nod. "I thought he made it up—but it affected me deeply. As he spoke the pain Amiele had caused me began to vanish. Instead I envisioned how gloriously I could now perform the role of the heartbroken heroine. How easily I could recreate the pain and bring an audience to tears. For the first time I understood that when I get up onstage and share an emotion with other people I bring us all closer. My sixteen-year-old soul was on fire. My purpose was clear. I would be an artist and work in the theater and touch people so that they would feel as deeply as I was feeling now. All that because of this stranger who never looked directly at me while he spoke."

"Did you ever see him again?" asks Ted.

"I looked for him the next day but no one knew who I was talking about. I never saw him again."

"He probably went back to Manhattan."

"Maybe," I reply.

"So that was your first experience with passion," says Ted.

"In this life anyway." I close my eyes and remember what it feels like to Jean as Franklin's hungry tongue presses against her lips and she opens her warm mouth to receive it. Her body goes limp with passion. Franklin's strong arms enfold and support her. She surrenders completely. The kiss. It is a kiss that I have known only in the foggiest, darkest hours of my deepest sleep. I put my hands to my heart. It's pounding so hard.

"It's Dennis, Ted. The man who loves me is Dennis."

"That's what I thought, Victoria."

"No, I mean in the Victorian times. The man that loves Jean is Dennis."

"It's 1998, Victoria." He grins, proud of himself. "You are living your own 'Victorian times' in your imagination."

Chapter Seven

I stand in front of my class the next day and find I can't speak. Shakespeare, you devil. The story of *Romeo and Juliet* seemed like fun when I proposed the idea of teaching a class on it last year. Today, it seems like a wicked, cosmic joke. Today, Satan and Shakespeare are in collusion to destroy my composure. I maintain a tenuous hold by teaching from my prepared notes, without expression, until most of the class time has passed. Then I hear myself say, "If Romeo and Juliet were to reincarnate today, what do you think their relationship would be?" The entrance of Dennis Manon as the question leaves my mouth is my answer.

"Maybe like Francesca and Robert Kincaid in *The Bridges of Madison County*," says Donna McKnight. I see Dennis grimace.

"Why is that?" I ask.

"Well, if suicide is a sin, maybe they would have to come back and long for each other but not be able to be together," she says.

A bit too sure of herself, I think. I say, "Do you believe suicide is a sin? Did Romeo and Juliet commit a sin?"

"Well, the Catholic Church—" says Donna.

She is interrupted by Tod Chilmark who says, "Give me a break, the Catholic Church!"

"Let's keep religion out of this," says another student tersely.

"Okay, okay, everyone, let's stay calm. What I want to know is, can lovers ever be happy if their passion overrides their social obligations?"

"No, 'cause the bills have to be paid and Romeo gets fat and bald, and Juliet loses her teeth, and Juliet has an affair and Romeo kills the lover and goes to prison," says Tod.

"So passion can't last?" I ask.

"I hope it does," says Laurie Metcalf, a beautiful girl in the front row.

I glance up at Dennis, who has taken a seat in the back of the room. Why is he here? I'm afraid to look at him. My silence continues for too long. "Professor Manon, what do you think?"

The students turn around in their seats to look at him and await his answer. His expression is guarded as he says, "Are you asking about passion or reincarnation?"

What am I asking? "Well, I'm just trying to make their love relevant to today. Is their story something we can relate to? Does passion still exist like that?" I desperately try to hold on.

"Obsessive love is universal and timeless. It usually ends in tragedy, though. Are these two lovers merely in love with love itself? Did Romeo really know Juliet? Did Juliet know Romeo? Was their passion fueled more by the restrictions against it?" He questions me calmly.

"Are you trying to say that it was Romeo and Juliet's obsession that destroyed them? It sounds as though you aren't acknowledging the usual romantic interpretation." My voice is tinged with anger.

"I don't mean to negate the romance. It wasn't only their single-minded obsessions that destroyed them. Society did its part. The families were at war and lines were drawn. Nobody was seeing very clearly."

"If everyone saw clearly we wouldn't have much of a story, would we?" I reply, sharply.

"No, I guess we wouldn't."

I glance down at my watch. My smile is strained and ugly. "Don't forget papers are due next week."

As the students leave, Dennis comes closer to me, "Victoria, sorry if I ruined your class."

"Oh, no, of course not," I say feeling patronized.

"How are you?" He touches my hand quickly—it seems an odd gesture.

I say, "Okay. And you?"

He nods. I pick up my books and we walk silently out of the room together. I head for my office, a place where we can shut the door and be alone. Dennis follows.

"Victoria?" Tom Banks calls to me from down the hall. I stop and turn as Tom hurries toward us.

"Tom, I want you to meet, Dennis Man…."

"Holy shit! It's the Man!" Tom reaches out his hand and grabs Dennis.

"And the Banker! How the hell are you? What are you doing here?" Dennis pulls Tom into him for a hug then shifts backward for a better look. Tom grins and shakes his head while Dennis laughs and hits him on the arm.

"Tom, I had no idea you were here. I thought you were teaching at Boston University. Last I heard."

"I'm doing a visiting professor stint," says Tom. "How about you?"

"I'm teaching in the English Department."

"You still with Rebecca?" asks Tom.

"We're married now," Dennis replies.

"The best man won," Tom says. "What are you doing this minute? Anything important? Got time for a beer?"

"Absolutely!"

I've been shifting uncomfortably from foot to foot. The overhead light in the hallway is out and I'm thankful that there is only one window at the far end of the corridor. The darkness makes me feel less awkward. My office is near the window and I glance toward it, wondering if I should leave quietly. "You know each other?"

They look at me. They had forgotten I was here.

"Oh, yeah. Dennis and I go back to college days. We both fell in love with the same woman. He won."

"Great," I say unconvincingly. "Did you want something, Tom?"

"Oh, yeah. About *The Maids*."

"You are doing *The Maids*? The original Theater of Pain, sado-masochistic, infuriate the audience production of *The Maids*?" asks Dennis.

"I live dangerously," says Tom. "You should know that. Remember our production of *Titus Andronicus*?"

"Shakespeare with black leather and chains?"

"The same." Tom laughs. "How do you know Victoria?"

"She rescued me," says Dennis.

"Good for her. Victoria, can we talk later? I'd love to have a beer with Dennis."

"Sure, no problem. You two reminisce about the old days."

"I'll talk to you later," Dennis says and claps his arm around Tom's shoulder. "Great to see you."

They walk, shoulder to shoulder away from me, into the gloomy hallway.

Chapter Eight

S o he acknowledged that something is going on between you?" Sally says to me a few days later over a cup of coffee at the local diner. The Moonglo diner is Sally's and my favorite breakfast spot. The blue vinyl seats are cracked and worn, the flowered curtains slightly yellowed and the menu features large platters of fried foods. She brushes her thick, red hair away from her face and reaches across the table to punch me in the arm. Sally is my best friend, despite her practical midwestern sensibilities and corn-fed philosophy. Originally from Indiana, she moved to Vermont ten years ago to attend college. After one year she dropped out and started working in an insurance office. That's how we met, over a homeowner's policy.

"No, not really. What he said is, 'You know I'm married. I have a child,'" I reply. "And he showed up at my class."

"And this tells you that you've known him in another life and you were lovers?" asks Sally.

"It's not what he said, it's how he said it. How he looks at me. The energy between us. And my visions." I feel like an idiot.

"I'm not sure I'm following you, Vicky. I mean, either you love someone or you don't. Take Jim and me. We broke up because he obviously wasn't in love with me enough to make babies and raise a family. At least that's how I see it," Sally says sensibly.

"How did we get to babies and a family? Come on, Sally, there are lots of ways to love someone. Wouldn't you agree?"

"Of course."

I sigh. "So Sally. Stretch a little here."

"I'm willing to stretch, but you've got to give me something besides a vision and a wedding ring." She grabs the waitress as she breezes by and orders a donut. "Anyway, what about Gary? I hope you haven't forgotten about him."

A stiletto of a question. "I haven't said anything to him about all this. In fact, I've been deliberately avoiding him until I figure out...."

"But all this reincarnation stuff is right up his alley."

"I know."

Sally sighs. "So what's your therapist say?"

I glance around the diner. The after-church crowd is just beginning to file in. The faces are pretty grim and I'm not comforted. I turn back to Sally. "Ted thinks I'm avoiding relationship problems with Gary by making this stuff up with Dennis."

"Well, he's a therapist. What do you expect?" A puzzled look. "Are you?"

"I'm not. I don't know what the hell this is, but it isn't Gary avoidance. I love him. Honest. In fact I'm going to tell him what's going on, about the visions. I swear it," I reply.

"These visions. Are they like pictures—hallucinations? Or dreams or ideas or what?"

"They're like memories, but vague. Some things are very clear, others almost impossible to retrieve. Like trying to remember a childhood birthday party, or your first date. You have a remembrance of how the people looked or how you felt when your boyfriend picked you up—whether you went to a dance or a movie. You can't say you actually see it, it's like you see it in your mind. Maybe more like a dream," I say.

"This past life, you're sure it's not just... I don't know, a subconscious fiction... you know, putting other faces on your own life?" asks Sally.

"Well, it doesn't match up at all," I begin. "I know that Jean married an older man, John Cobb, I think his name is. He was wealthy and kind, but the love felt more like a father-daughter or brother-sister love than the passionate love of a husband and wife. I know that the man—his name is Franklin—was my husband's friend and he fell deeply in love with Jean. They had an affair...." I trail off and my focus blurs.

I signal the waitress for more coffee. When she brings it and refills my cup I don't pause to keep the conversation private, but continue talking, regardless of what she thinks.

"I snuck out of the house, pretending to visit a friend or a sick aunt, and boldly entered his home, even in the light of day. Oh my God, Sally! The sex. It was marvelous. I mean there was something so sinful it gave an added thrill to the chemistry that is already there. Undressing was an art!"

The waitress lingers over my cup of coffee, eager to hear more. I glance up at her and she reluctantly moves slowly.

"Corsets, hairpins and starched collars were removed between frantic kisses. I can still remember what it felt like as his hands slid down my leg to remove my stockings. We weren't shy. I always thought Victorians made love like sixteen-year-olds afraid of losing their virginity. Franklin certainly didn't. There wasn't a part of my body his lips didn't taste."

Sally and I simultaneously let out an enormous sigh and fall back into our seats.

"I have to leave now, my love," I say to him.

He does not reply. We have done this so many other times.

"They are expecting me at home."

He glares at me. "To hell with them! They don't love you as I do. Why should you return to him, and to his children, when your heart and the man you love is here?"

"Because I am married to him."

"And yet you are in bed with me."

I recoil and tears fill my eyes.

His face registers my pain. "I'm sorry, Jean. I love you so much. I can't bear this anymore. Please don't cry."

"Do you think this is easy for me? Do you think I am happy for one moment in this cursed existence?" I spit the words at him. "I must go." I feel imprisoned by my life.

He grabs at me, tugging at the corset I am attempting to secure around my torso. "Please. We can run away to America together. We can leave him."

"John's children," I say. "They have lost one mother. If I leave they would lose another one. How can I do this?"

"How can you not?"

I continue to dress as the tears run down my face. It is far worse than even he suspects; if he looked carefully he would notice that my corset was not fitting as before. I fear I am with child....

...A minute of silence passes before Sally breaks it. "So, what happens? Were you pregnant? My God, Vicky, you can't leave me here!"

"Well," I say. "I only know one other part. You want to hear it?" The eager look on her face has already given me the answer. She nods.

I sit back and close my eyes to bring the scene into focus....

My husband, John, sits before the fire in the master bedroom. He reads, smokes his pipe and doesn't notice I have opened the door a crack to observe him. I walk quietly over to his chair.

"It is chilly this evening," I say. "I made certain a fire was burning in the children's room. They should be warm enough tonight."

"Come sit with me," he says and indicates the chair across from him. "I am happy to have your company. We see each other so rarely these days. Your sick aunt takes up all your time. How is she?"

I can't look him in the eye. I've been using my aunt as an excuse to visit Franklin. "Not well, but she hangs on to life with a strong passion."

"Give her my regards."

"I always do." A silence descends which presses against my temples. "I have something to tell you."

"Yes?"

"We are going to have a child." I speak in almost a whisper.

"A baby?"

"Yes. I hope you don't mind."

"A baby? This is wonderful news. Mind? Why should I mind, my dearest Jean?" He rises from his chair and pulls me to my feet to embrace me strongly. "Thanks be to God. A child of our own. I love you so, Jean. You are such a devoted mother to my children. Our child will be so loved and cared for. It is truly happy news!"

His innocence cuts me like a knife....

..."You must feel like shit," Sally interrupts. "Especially in that day and age."

"I did. I do. You know what I mean."

I am confused. My guilt and anguish have made me believe that John will be angry with me for being pregnant. On some level I have forgotten that he knows nothing of the affair. "I was afraid you might not want another child," I say to him.

"What are you saying? Of course a child is wonderful. Why would it be otherwise?" John looks at me with surprise.

I am comforted by his reaction. "No reason. I am happy too."

He walks me to the bed and holds me in his arms. "I am sorry if I have not had the time to spend with you I might like. My poor, serious Jean. You mustn't worry so. When my wife died I never thought I would love again. I know I do not tell you often enough how I feel. I am a man of few words in my home and too many words in my work. Jean, you have given my life meaning again."

He speaks gently and with such compassion that I can't bear to look at him.

"Oh John, I will try to be a good wife and mother for you."

"There, there, my darling. Rest now."

He lays me in the bed and sits with me for an hour rocking me and stroking my head. The demons of guilt, shame and betrayal swarm around me....

"Well that's it," I say, breathing out a sigh of relief.

Sally scrunches up her eyes and shakes her head back and forth a few times. "I was going to tell you about my date last night, but now it seems pretty stupid and inconsequential."

I nod in agreement and glance out the window of the diner. Dennis is walking in. "Oh my God! He's here!" I sink down low in the booth, feeling immediately fifteen again.

"He's a good-looking guy," Sally says. She knows immediately who he is. "And I think he's not alone. Looks like his wife and child are with him."

I can't resist the temptation to turn around in the seat and peek over the edge of the booth as they enter the restaurant. He doesn't notice me and escorts his family to another part of the diner.

"Methinks she's pregnant," Sally says calmly.

"What? Maybe she's just... chunky."

"Hardly. I should be so lucky to look like that and I'm not even pregnant."

I have to admit she's right. She looks pregnant. Very. Lots of stomach, but the rest of her is thin. For a pregnant lady she is certainly graceful. They are dressed up and it looks like they've come from church. The daughter is beautiful. Must be four or five. Blonde, sweet face, the works. "Shit! Shit! Shit!"

"Shit is sure shootin'."

"Let's go."

Sally nods. I run out the front door and make her stand at the cashier and pay the check. Suddenly I feel like I need a cigarette. It would be my first in four years.

Chapter Nine

*S*moke enters my lungs, satisfying every inch of my body and soul. I've been smoking for three days, long enough for it to feel really good again. An old coffee cup has been turned into a makeshift ashtray on my desk. Two cigarette butts occupy the bottom, and the third one in my hand covers them with ashes.

Term papers stare up at me. I promised to return them today. I flip through the remaining; five to go. I glance up at the clock. It's almost time for Dennis's class. Should I go or not? I rise from my seat, like a sleepwalker, and make my way to his classroom. By the time I get there he's in full swing. I sneak inside—Dennis notices. I detect a slight wobble in his voice. I sit down quietly in the back row. Sweat beads up on my forehead and palms. So, he didn't tell me she was pregnant. He didn't owe me that. What am I thinking?

I want to leave, but I'm afraid because then he'll know that I'm upset and I couldn't bear to stay. I'm afraid to stay because I feel so unhinged and I realize I'm not sure if I can put on a brave face. I need some fresh air. I need a cigarette. I hurry to the student union for coffee, cigarettes and breath mints.

I have another hour until my class and I still have those five papers to grade. I force myself back to the office and decide to give them all B's. Then my conscience overtakes me and I decide to try and read each one of them and give them the mark they deserve. Feeling buoyed by coffee and cigarettes, I even make a few clever remarks on the margin. I know that five papers in an hour is really pushing it, but I try anyway. By the time I get to my class I am a nervous wreck and I'm sure the students can sense it.

"I'm sorry to say that I graded all but two papers," I say sheepishly. "Would you like me to return the ones I graded and the other two can get theirs at my office later today?"

"Yes!" the resounding answer comes from the class. I return the papers and apologize to the two who sit empty handed.

"Take a minute and look at the papers. If you have any questions or any thoughts you want to bring up for discussion after reviewing my comments you may do so."

The students sit in silence, and I stare out the window onto the campus, through the trees, and let my mind wander until it ends up back at Dennis's classroom.

"Ahem." A student clears his voice and brings me back to earth. "I have a question."

"Yes?"

"How come I got a C?" he asks.

"Talk to me about that later. This is for specific questions, not just to go over the entire paper and justify the grade."

"Well, I want you to know I'm pissed about this grade," he says.

"Understood. We'll talk about it later." I sit in silence for another moment when BAM! All of a sudden, my heart starts beating wildly and my throat closes up. In my mind's eye I see Jean racing down cobblestone streets in the pouring rain. I feel the blood drain from my face.

"Ms. Barkley," a student says. "Are you okay? You look really pale all of a sudden."

"I think I might have eaten something bad. I feel quite ill. I'd better go lie down."

I run from the room with the words, "But when can we discuss this paper?" at my back.

When I was given tenure I moved into an office big enough to accommodate a couch and right now I bless it as I stretch out. I put a pillow over my face and rock back and forth. What the hell is Jean doing? Running in the rain? She's running after someone. She is desperate....

The cobblestones are slippery and rain pours in rivulets between the grooves. Her dress is wet and heavy as she pulls it upward out of the mud. Her arms are tired from the strain of lifting the layers of fabric.

"Franklin! Don't leave me! Please don't leave!" She slips and falls but manages to right herself and continue onward. She brushes a strand of hair from her face and lifts her gaze from the street. A carriage is pulling away in the distance.

"Franklin! Don't leave me! I love you!"

She is shoved from behind. She falls to the ground and looks up to see her husband staring down at her. "Let me go!" she cries as he grabs her arm to pull her up out of the mud.

"He is gone, Jean. He left for America."

"No! He loves me."

"Come home, Jean. He is gone."

The shame is palpable. I feel it in every pore of my body. Shame, regret, disgust, heartbreak—and more. Guilt, anguish, love. The emotions overwhelm me. I feel Jean; I know her. I may not understand every detail of her life, or know every moment of her existence, but Goddammit, I know how she feels. I recognize it. And I know she is me. Not a figment of my imagination. Fuck Ted. Fuck everyone else. Fuck all of you. This is real. It has to be.

KNOCK! KNOCK! I jump.

"Who is it?"

"It's Tom."

"Oh, Tom. Just a minute." I pull the pillow from my face. Still dazed I stand up and walk to the door. "Hi, Tom." A look of embarrassment crosses his face and I realize that I must look pretty rough and have mascara smudged under my eyes.

"Is this a bad time?"

"Come on in." I stand aside and give him room to enter. I sit at my desk and reach for a cigarette.

"I didn't know you smoked," he says.

"I don't." I light the cigarette and offer him one.

"No, thanks. I quit about a year ago."

"I quit four years ago."

"I can see that." He winces, starts to speak, then remains quiet.

I can't look at him. Don't know why... except that he is good friends with Dennis. He apparently lost out to him for Rebecca's affections. I blow a paltry smoke ring, turn to him. "Tom, do you believe in reincarnation?"

It is obviously the last question he expected to hear. "I—I don't know. I haven't thought that much about it."

My head bounces with several nods.

"I've managed to avoid thinking too much about the after life. I figure I'll find out soon enough." His eyes narrow. "Why do you ask?"

"Well, I do. I really, really, really do. I didn't know that I did until I met Dennis. But now I'm sure of it." I take a deep drag off my cigarette and pull out a tissue and wipe the circles under my eyes.

"Dennis?" Tom raises his eyebrows. He looks elfin when he does that.

"Yes, Dennis. Your old college buddy."

"Is that what's bothering you?" he asks.

It is a far more direct question than I expected. Truthfully I'm not sure of the answer. "Indirectly I guess he's the cause. But not in this life."

"Not in this life," he repeats. "This is getting a bit too heavy for me. I came to talk about *The Maids*. I already got a call from an irate parent. Barney, the actor that plays Claire—his father is real pissed. Turns out he's a born again something and it's over his dead body that his son is going to play a woman. I explained to him that his son was of legal age, but to no avail. We got a real piece of work on our hands."

"I'm sure it will be all right. Tom, is Dennis happily married?"

"I can't say I honestly know. I assume so. Married men are even more dangerous than directing a Genet play, Victoria. Stay away."

"I am. I just wondered. I loved him so much one hundred and forty years ago. I had his baby, you know."

"His baby?"

I nod.

Tom's face registers his confusion. "Listen, Victoria, I don't want to be in the middle of anything."

"Tom, there's no middle to be in."

"What should I do about this angry parent?"

"What can you do? Let Barney handle it. It's his father, he's had to deal with it all his life."

"Okay."

He stands up to leave, and I sense his relief that he is going to be getting out of my office.

"Bye, Tom."

"Will I see you at rehearsal tomorrow night?" he asks.

"I'll stop by."

"Thanks." He shuts the door behind him.

In the silence that follows his departure I realize I now have another emotion to add to the ones already overwhelming me. I feel like an asshole.

Chapter Ten

I roll over in Gary's bed and peek out under the shade to squint at the morning. The grass is brown, the trees are brown and the sky is gray. The monotone sight makes me feel empty. As though the Earth resigned its position—it just gave up and walked away, leaving me in a colorless void.

I turn in bed to face the other direction and see Gary's meditation alcove where he retreats nearly everyday for contemplation. A fat-bellied Buddha grins at me. I imagine his earlobes growing bigger and bigger until, like Dumbo the elephant, he can take off and fly around the room. The only thing I've ever liked about religion is the theatrics. To me it's a bunch of bowing and scraping to something you can't see but are supposed to take on "faith." The concept of God reminds me of an improvisation assignment in an acting class. For example, the teacher might say, imagine you are trapped in a crippled submarine and losing oxygen. There's no submarine, no ocean, plenty of oxygen but somehow if you do it well enough you can convince the other actors in the room you are surrounded by a nuclear submarine, at the bottom of the ocean, suffocating to death. Buddha seems to enjoy my foolish thoughts. I swear his grin just increased and he winked at me. "I'm going to tell him," I say.

"Tell him what?" Gary mumbles.

I draw in a deep breath to steady myself. Gary rises on his elbows and gives me a quick kiss.

"Tell me what?"

"Gary, do you believe in reincarnation?"

"You know I do. Why?" He smiles gently at me, sensing my fear.

"I'm having some past life visions. At least that's what I think they are." I wiggle around in the bed to put distance between us. "I guess I haven't said anything because I'm not sure what I'm feeling. I've been so confused and uncertain lately."

"That would explain your distant behavior. I've barely seen you in the past month," he says.

He doesn't say it meanly so I try not to get defensive. I merely whisper, "Sorry."

"What are the visions about?"

I close my eyes and remember Jean entering Franklin's bedroom for the first time. I can feel his arm around her shoulder as he leads her to the bed and cradles her gently.

How deeply Franklin is contained in Jean's heart. I remember the kiss that frees her soul and releases the playful child in her, until their frolicking and rolling ends with her on top of him. Finally, I see through her eyes as she looks down at him beneath her, and I witness the love that pours out from his eyes. I understand that it is Franklin who sets Jean free by loving her to the very depths of her being—adoring, and passionate.

"They are about Victorian lovers."

"How literary," he says.

"Don't make fun of me, Gary. I don't think I can take it."

"How come you're having visions?"

I never thought out about having to actually answer that question. In my fantasies Gary would ask about the past life stuff and then he'd understand completely and then I'd feel better. I didn't actually think I'd have to explain Dennis to him. "Well, I met a man. I think he is the reason I'm discovering the lovers. He's triggering these visions."

I feel Gary's muscles tense up next to me. I glance over in time to see his jaw tighten. He gets up slowly and puts on a black silk robe adorned with white Chinese characters. He raises the shade and stands next to the window to look out. I imagine him a lonely Tibetan monk, meditating on the deeper spiritual meaning of life.

"Gary?" I interrupt his reverie. He doesn't answer. Again, silence for another few minutes. There are a million things I could say: he's married—we haven't done anything. They all seem childlike, silly and irrelevant. I pick at a loose thread in the comforter.

"Do you love him?" Gary asks without turning around.

The question frightens me. Nobody else has asked me that. "I don't know." I throw the comforter over my head. "It's just a past life vision," I say without lifting the covers.

"So why are you hiding?" I can picture the serious expression on his face as he says this.

Why am I hiding? "It's just that Jean loves Franklin so much. She's married to someone else, but she's pregnant with Franklin's baby and then Franklin leaves her. After he leaves she realizes she should have gone with him instead of staying with her husband."

"I don't mean to diminish this, Victoria, but have you been reading *Jane Eyre*?"

I pop my head out from underneath the covers just long enough to say, "Fuck you."

"Okay. Let's start this again. You are having past life visions that are being triggered by someone you know now. Who is he?" he asks again.

"His name is Dennis Manon. He is an English professor at the college." I say it quietly, half-hoping the covers will muffle my voice enough so he can't hear me.

"Okay," he draws the word out as though the mere saying of it stretches his patience.

I lift the cover from my head and say, "I don't know much more."

"Does this affect your feelings for me?"

"Absolutely not."

"It's affected you this deeply, but it hasn't affected our relationship," he says with a cynical tone to his voice. "Have you talked to your therapist about it?" he asks.

"Fuck my therapist. You're smarter than he is."

"Have you been ducking him for the past month also?"

"No."

"I see." Gary stands up and walks to a bookshelf. There are four floor-to-ceiling bookshelves in his bedroom and another twelve spread out between the living room and his study. "You say the emergence of these past lives hasn't affected our relationship?" He kneels and runs his fingers over the books. "It would seem that the only thing it has affected is our relationship."

I take the time to jump out of the bed and run naked to the cold bathroom. I'm shivering on the toilet, my arms wrapped around my body for warmth.

"You ever heard of karma?" Gary calls through the door.

"Don't patronize me, Gary. Don't make fun of me. I'm sorry I brought this up at all." I flush the toilet, scurry into the bedroom and jump back under the covers.

"Karma comes around in its own time. This life or another life—there is karma lurking in this tale of yours."

"Gary, this isn't some abstract Buddhist idea of reincarnation I'm experiencing. This is very specific torture. This is visceral. This is in my guts, my heart and my soul. It's not going to be resolved or understood by reading or sitting at some altar and meditating about it." I get back out of bed, grab my underpants lying on the floor and pull them on. Then I reach for my jeans, suck in my stomach and zip them up.

"Are you saying that I'm not capable of understanding this past life of yours?" he asks. His brow wrinkles and he frowns at me. "Hell, I'm a Buddhist."

"I'm not sure that just being a Buddhist means a person is ready to experience what I'm going through." It occurs to me suddenly that perhaps I don't want him to be so understanding. This is messy and ugly and all too human. I want someone to understand my suffering, by knowing inside and out exactly how I'm feeling. Maybe some part of me also wants to pick a fight.

"So you are in love with him."

"This is not about whether or not I am in love with anyone." I throw my sweater on and sit down on the bed to put on my socks and shoes. I just hope I can make it to the door before either of us says anything permanently damaging. "Everything always seems so easy to you, Gary. You're so damn rational."

"Karma is rational. It's Universal Law."

"Fuck Universal Law."

"That's like saying, 'Fuck God.' "

"Why don't you go live in a temple? I've got to leave." Over his shoulder I see Buddha. He hasn't changed one bit—he is still grinning at me.

My car turns the corner by my house and immediately I am aware of about ten people standing on the Pi Gamma Delta lawn— all over the age of forty. The young sorority sisters are sticking their heads out of open windows on the second floor and watching them. What's really odd about the scene is that the older people are carrying white poster board signs on sticks. Most of the signs aren't raised in the air, but hanging by their legs. I slow down to try and read them. Mrs. Thompson is carrying one that reads: HO-MOSEXUALITY IS SINFUL. Who is homosexual and why are they protesting? Did Mrs. Thompson discover two of the sorority sisters naked in bed?

Standing next to Mrs. Thompson is her friend from the restaurant—the man with the slicked back hair and the bolo tie. His sign reads: ST GEORGE COLLEGE: HOME TO THE DEVIL. Holy Shit! What is this? I slow down and pull into my driveway next to them. Mrs. Thompson raises her hand and points her finger at me. Then she runs toward the car waving her sign in the air. The others follow. Before I can get out of the car I am surrounded.

"You are responsible for that sinful production being shown at the college," Mrs. Thompson yells at me through the car window.

"What are you talking about?" I scream back at her.

"*The Maids*," screams the man. "My son is on stage wearing a dress and prancing around. I want it stopped, now!"

"What the hell am I supposed to do?" I shout at him. I'm afraid to open the window even a crack.

"Stop it! You are a director in the Theater department. Stop it!" Mrs. Thompson screams again.

"I can't!" I shout and put the car in reverse. Slowly I back up, honking and honking and honking. "I'll run over your feet," I scream. "Get out of my way!" Once I make it to the street I head for the college, slowly at first until the protesters tire and I can race away. I'm shaking and I don't know how to feel. It's funny and horrifying all at once. Does Tom know about this? The show opens tonight.

I run to the Theater Arts department and directly into the Chairman's office without knocking. I bend over and brace my hands on my thighs to catch my breath. It's eight-thirty on Friday morning. I'm wearing jeans, an old sweater, my face isn't washed, and my hair isn't brushed. My breath smells terrible and I had an early morning fight about Buddhism with my boyfriend followed by a run-in with the Christian Right.

George glances up and frowns. "Victoria? Are you all right?"

"They're all over my lawn. With signs about the show and homosexuality," I gasp.

"What are you talking about?"

"The actor's father. What's his name? Barney. Barney's father is pissed. They want us to close the show."

"So? What's new? The world is nuts," he says.

"So? I've got a lawn full of maniacs. They will be all over us in a matter of minutes. They will be all over you!"

"What can we do? Stop the play?" asks George.

"I don't know. But I want them off my lawn. It's not even my production."

"I'll talk to Tom. It's his play after all. This is precisely why I gave the directing job to him." George picks up the phone and dials. "He's not in his office. I'll try him at home."

I sit down in a chair and collapse. "This sucks. This really sucks."

"Tom, it's George. Listen, I've got Victoria in my office. She says her yard is full of protesters. They want the play stopped. I think it's being led by Barney's father."

Silence. "Okay, thanks." George hangs up the phone.

"He'll be right over. He'll meet us here. Why don't you go and get yourself a cup of coffee at the student union."

"I'll be back in a bit." I smooth down my rat's nest of hair and sigh. "I really don't need this."

"You and me both," says George. "Should be a doozy of an opening night."

***

It's five o'clock and the actors are huddled in their dressing room. Barney has been crying. Michael and Chris, the other actors, look terrified. Michael, who plays Madame, is sitting next to Barney trying to comfort him. Michael is small-boned and delicate and he gently strokes Barney's shoulder.

"My Dad is crazy. That's why my Mom divorced him. He's nuts. He used to beat me with a… I know he can't hurt me anymore, but Goddammit, why doesn't he leave me alone!" Barney pounds his fist into the counter and stares into the mirror. "You don't know, Mr. Banks, he's nuts. He can get violent."

I'm standing around to lend support, even though there isn't much I can do.

"What do you want to do, Barney?" asks Tom. "Just name it."

"I don't know, part of me wants to say, 'Fuck Him,' and part of me wants to run away." Barney stands up and paces the room. His hair has been pushed away from his face and is plastered down tightly against his head to allow for a wig. He's wearing sweatpants, a St. George's sweatshirt, high-heels and has on heavy white face powder to cover a slight beard. In heels he's six foot two inches tall and he looks pretty scary even as terrified as he seems.

"What's this really about, Barney?" asks Chris, his castmate. "Is it about being gay? Come on. Everyone knows you're gay. Everyone knows I'm gay. Michael is straight and everyone thinks he's gay because he took this ridiculous part in this ridiculous play."

"It's not about being gay. It's about being scared."

"What's your Dad going to do?" I ask. "What can he do to you? I mean, yeah, he's threatened by a play that's pretty strange, but so what? You don't talk to him anyway, right?"

"I try not to. He's convinced I'm working for the Devil and he sees it as his moral duty to convert me," says Barney.

"Are you serious?" says Michael.

"Dead serious. My Dad takes this stuff ultra-seriously," says Barney. He lights a cigarette.

"Can I have one of those?" I ask.

"Sure." Barney slides the pack down the counter toward me. Tom intercepts it.

"I think I'll take one of those too," Tom says and pulls the Marlboro out of the pack and puts it to his lips. Barney leans over and lights the cigarette for him.

"Look at me, the Marlboro Man," says Barney, and laughs for the first time all afternoon.

Tom hands the pack to me. "So we both fell off the wagon."

"At this point I feel morally justified," I reply and put one to my lips. Barney lights mine as well.

"Okay, it's decision time. Are you going out there or not?" asks Tom.

"Let's do it," says Barney. "Fuck him. He's an asshole."

It's 7:45 and there isn't a poster board sign or Christian fundamentalist in sight. Barney is backstage pacing furiously. Word has gotten out on campus about Barney's father and Pi Gamma Delta's Mrs. Thompson and the theater is full. This play would have been difficult to sell if it hadn't been for the rumors.

"Where is he?" asks Barney. "I don't trust him."

"He probably gave up," I say. "He realized that he was helping to fill seats rather than keep people away."

"I doubt it," says Barney.

"Two minutes to curtain," says Tom. "You okay, Barney?"

"I'm fine."

"Places everyone. Break a leg," Tom says and hurries offstage. I've decided to stand in the wings with him to give him support. I reach over and squeeze his hand. "It's going to be okay," I whisper. I peek my face out and see Dennis in the first row. Gary is sitting three rows behind him. I take a deep breath.

The curtain opens on Barney, as the housemaid named Claire. He's wearing a black slip, his back is to a dressing table and he extends his hand in an exaggerated gesture. Although he's tall, there is something very graceful about his movements. With the fake breasts, wig and makeup I almost believe the transformation is permanent. Claire is making fun of the mistress of the house known as Madame by imitating her behavior.

CLAIRE: Those gloves! Those gloves! I've told you time and again to leave them in the kitchen. You probably hope to seduce the milkman with them. No, no, don't lie; that won't get you any-where! Hang them over the sink. When will you understand that this room is not to be sullied. Everything, yes, everything that comes out of the kitchen is spit! So stop it! Make yourself quite at home. Preen like a peacock. And above all, don't hurry, we've plenty of time. Go!

Claire is talking to Solange, another housemaid. Claire sits down at the dressing table, sniffs some flowers, runs her hands over the toilet articles, brushes her hair and pats her face.

CLAIRE: Get my dress ready. Quick! Time presses. Are you there?

A shot rings out. Barney falls to the floor. Chris stares at Barney. For thirty seconds nobody moves. Then Tom rushes onto the stage. Barney has fallen backwards; blood gushes from his chest.

"He's been shot!" screams Tom. "Call an ambulance." The theater erupts in screams. I race out onto the stage just as another shot sounds in the audience.

In a daze I walk to the edge of the stage and peer out to see what happened. Standing between the front row of seats and the stage is Mrs. Thompson. She pulls the dark glasses she used as a disguise from her face and looks up into my eyes. "This is your fault," she screams at me. "You and the rest of you… you actors!" She spits the word at me like a curse. Then she turns and races up the aisle toward the exit, pushing and shoving her way through the panicked crowd.

Lying face-up about a foot from where Mrs. Thompson had been standing is Barney's father—I recognize him even with the goatee he used to obscure his identity. His scalp is partially re-moved. A miniature statue of Jesus is lying on the floor next to a handgun.

Dennis has risen from his seat in the front row and kneels over the body. I jump down off the stage and stand next to him, being careful to avert my eyes from the half-opened skull. Dennis picks up the statue of Jesus and lifts it to me in his trembling hand. His eyes look hollow and his mouth is gaping. His expression frightens me as much as the bloody body on the floor. Suddenly I feel very sick and I stumble backstage to the bathroom.

Chapter Eleven

My horses hooves pound out dusty blasts with violent, powerful strokes on the dry, parched earth beneath them. Bodies pour from their homes onto the streets—panicked mothers clutch babies and children, eyes wide to witness the fierce invaders who have swept down upon them in their search for slaves.

Fallen bodies cover the ground. Their limbs hacked and covered in blood. A young boy kneels beside the body of his mother. Blood runs from her throat; her eyes stare motionless to the sky. Rampaging horses, and the screaming, strangled throat cries of other victims surround the kneeling boy, but he doesn't move. He stares at me, begging me with his eyes to help. I stop my horse and gaze at his trembling form....

I awaken with a scream. My body feels heavy and thick. Where am I? My heart is pounding and I sit up in bed and look around the room. For a moment I don't recognize anything. All of the things surrounding me belong to someone else. I look at the charcoal sketches thumb tacked into the wall. Who did those? I close my eyes. The face of a young boy kneeling beside his murdered mother returns to me. I snap my eyes open, afraid to see it again. I remember Dennis's expression as he kneeled beside Barney's dead father. Tears come, slowly at first. Then the dam breaks and I howl with sadness and rage.

A loud knock on the door breaks into my consciousness. I don't want to answer it. I peek out the living room window and see two men standing on my doorstep. They look official. I decide I'd better let them in.

"Yes?" I say meekly. I wipe my eyes and nose on my sleeve.

"Victoria Barkley?" one of them asks.

"Yes," I reply.

"This is Detective Madison. I'm Detective Denning. Can we come in?"

"Certainly." I step aside.

"We won't take up much of your time. We know you witnessed what appears to be a murder-suicide and we need to ask you a few questions."

I wrap my old robe closer around me and sit down on the couch. "Have a seat," I say. They do.

"Barney was a brilliant actor, a wonderful person. He had lots of friends and was well liked by the faculty," I say. "But, I only met his father when he picketed on my lawn that morning carrying a sign that read HOMOSEXUALS ARE THE DEVIL'S HELPMATES or some such nonsense."

"He picketed on your lawn?" asks Detective Denning.

"Oh, yes. He was upset because his son, Barney, was going to be playing the part of a woman in a play. But really the person you should be talking to is Mrs. Thompson from next door. She was also one of the people picketing on my lawn. She's the sorority mother and she and Barney's father were good friends, I saw her in the theater the night of the murder. It seems to me that Mrs. Thompson will have a lot of information. She might have even known the murderer's intentions beforehand." There. I did it. I paid the old witch back.

On Wednesday I attend the memorial for Barney. It is packed; even people who didn't know him have come to pay their respects. In the front row, the students of the theater department sit, men wearing women's clothing, women wearing men's. A number of people speak about freedom and tolerance—religious, sexual, artistic—one speech blends into the next until Barney's mother walks to the podium to speak. Thankfully she had been absent from the theater the night Barney was shot. I don't know how she has the strength to stand up before the crowd. She is silent for about two or three minutes. She dabs a tissue to her eyes and nose. I wonder if she will turn around and walk back to her seat without saying a word. Finally, she takes a deep breath and speaks.

"I came here with so much anger and pain," she begins. "And now that I'm up here I don't think there is anything I can say to express the way I'm feeling. I loved my son with all my heart, and I was extremely proud of the person he had… was becoming." She lets her eyes roam over the front row. "I thank all of you for your show of love as well." Her shoulders start to stoop; then she catches herself and straightens. "Don't let them win, or my son's death will have been for nothing." Everyone in the room starts to cry and it is over.

Dust lies everywhere, coating the feet, legs, even the throats of the citizens of Rome. "Citizens" refers to the men, for although women exist here, men move about much more freely, collecting the filth and grime in every crease and pit of their bodies. The art of bathing is a ritual shared by men and one that I am, today, for the first time, to be introduced to by my father. He drags my gangly limbs up stone steps. His hands are brutishly powerful, and twist painfully into the soft skin of my upper arm. I am aware, as he hauls me into this place, that I dare not disobey him. To do so would mean physical punishment, perhaps death.

A woman appears, a gentle and foreign creature, and she washes our hands and faces to remove the dirt caked there. My nervous eagerness finds solace in the warmth of her smile. It is fleeting, for my father has none of this gentle quality to his nature, and when my attention returns to him I notice a low trembling inside me. Roughly he pulls me away from her and into a large room with high ceilings. In the center of the room is a pool of water. White marble columns and murals on the walls serve as decoration. Men drape their bodies about. Some are lying propped up on their side by an elbow. A few lie on their backs with their hands beneath their heads, while others sit together in small groups. Their voices seem very loud to me, and they echo off the water and the walls. Although a few of the boys are teenagers, I am the youngest. Only eight years old, my body is still that of a child—completely hairless.

Across the room is a man. I notice him immediately. Even at eight years of age I sense something dangerous about him. When he stares at my father his eyes glow with fire and his face hardens. As my father draws closer to him I feel his hands and arms grow tense. His grip hurts me. My father stops before the man. They stare at one another without speaking. My father releases the grip on my hand. "He is yours for the afternoon. I will return." Without another word my father turns to go. I am alone.

I'm sure of it now. I'm going mad. I went back to bed after the memorial service and picked up my sketchpad. I wanted to sketch my dream—the one of the Roman soldiers and the young boy kneeling beside his mother. I drew three pictures of the scene in my mind, all of them terrifying.

Then I drew the Roman baths. I didn't know I had that image in my head, but it came out through my hand. I am trembling now. Feeling the fear of the young boy. Knowing intuitively what is to happen to him. Knowing, perhaps, what the young boy did not know—that he is to be pleasure for this man. A sexual slave won by this man in a contest.

"Dennis?" I knock on his door and peek in my head when I hear a faint, "Yes."

"Hi, Dennis. It's Victoria."

"Hey. Come on in. I was about to go home."

"How are you doing?" I step into the room.

"Okay. I was just sitting here thinking about Barney's memorial service."

"It was very moving."

"It was." I don't sit down. He doesn't offer. We both stare at each other. It seems we are both thinking about the same thing—Barney's dead father and his blown off skull. "Want to get a drink?"

"Yes, please."

"Anywhere in particular?" I ask.

"Somewhere where there are fewer students," he says, echoing my thoughts.

"Across town. You follow me in your car. Okay?"

"You're on." He grabs his coat and puts his hand on my back as he ushers me from his office and locks the door.

The late October wind whips around us, adding to my already sharpened senses. Halloween is tomorrow. I take him to a bar across town that Sally and I like to frequent, called Mike's Place.

"Ever been here?" I ask.

"Can't say I have," he says as we enter the dingy hole-in-the-wall and the smell of stale beer and cigarettes assaults our nostrils. "No danger of seeing anybody we know here."

"In a small town it's hard to get away." I take his hand and usher him past the only other couple in the place to a dark booth. He lets me hold his hand until we separate to sit across from each other. We wait for a minute in silence before we realize that a waitress is never going to appear. Dennis offers to get the beer and I watch him closely as he walks up to the bar to get two drafts. I have an overwhelming urge to light a cigarette but suppress it. He smiles as he sits back into the booth and scoots the beer across the table in front of me.

"So," he says. "How are you?"

I look down at the beer, take a sip and find I have no idea how to respond. Instead I let out a big sigh.

"It's tough. I've been having a terrible time with it. Barney's dad, lying there dead in front of me. It's haunting me. I can't believe he did it. How do you kill your own son?" says Dennis.

"Fathers do a lot of horrible things to their sons."

"Maybe so. But it isn't everyday I witness it first hand." Dennis takes a large gulp of his beer. He looks at me and I see that tears have formed in his eyes and threaten to spill over.

"Dennis, I need to talk to you. I don't have a clue how I'm going to go about this. I only know that I have to say something." I feel sick. "Do you mind if I smoke?"

Dennis shakes his head. "No, go ahead. That hard, huh?"

I nod, reach into my purse and withdraw a cigarette.

He reaches out his hand and touches mine. Gently his fingers linger and caress me.

His touch is like a magnet. It draws the words from me. "Dennis, I think we've known one another in a past life."

He looks at me with a wry smile. "What does that mean?"

"It means that we've been together before this life. It means we've had other lives. It means we're connected. It means I'm having visions that I don't completely understand. And it means I'm attracted to you."

I don't want to hear him say he's married, so I rush on. "I've been having these visions about the Victorian times. A woman and man who aren't married, but love each other desperately. I believe I was that woman and you were the man. We couldn't marry because I was already married. But we had an affair. And I got pregnant with your child."

Dennis looks at me. "How do I respond to that?"

"I don't know if there is anything you can say. But I know it's real. Do you want me to tell you more about it?"

"Sure. I guess so. Can I have one of those?" He points to my cigarette.

"I didn't know you smoked."

"I don't. Not since college."

I reach into my purse and withdraw an ultra light cigarette. "It's not macho enough to kill you instantly," I say. "I just started back after years off of them myself."

He lights the cigarette. Coughs a few times. Takes a swig of beer. I get the feeling he doesn't really want to know the rest of the story. "You know I'm married," he says.

He has to say it. "Of course, I know you are married. Dennis, this isn't about that. This is something else. Something bigger than right here, right now. Something that has led us here to be together sharing these experiences," I say.

"I think I understand."

"I'm talking about karma," I say. "What comes around goes around."

"You think we have… karma?" he asks.

"Maybe. What I know is that in a past life you were named Franklin and I was named Jean and we fell madly in love and broke each other's hearts."

Dennis looks at me as though the world contains only the two of us. My body swells with feelings too enormous to be held within my cells. His eyes become dark tunnels to the center of my soul and I force myself to look deeply into them.

"Victoria." he whispers.

"Dennis?" I say quietly.

"Listen, I think I'd better go."

"I'm sorry."

"Oh, no. Please. It's not you. Well, it is you. But it's not what you think. Well, maybe it is what you think. What do you think?" he asks.

"What do I think? I think you think I'm out of my mind and you can't wait to get away."

"I don't. Not at all. I think I'd better go," he says as he rises from the booth and heads for the door.

I watch him, feeling like a revealed fool with a red face—dumbfounded, deserted, angry. He turns around, comes back to the booth, leans over and kisses me. On the lips but without opening his mouth.

"Bye," he says and gives me a look that melts my heart.

"Bye." I smile bravely and wave as he runs out the door. I sit for a moment in silence, then reach for my cigarettes. I light one up and take a deep, deep drag off the wrong end.

Chapter Twelve

My body is changing. Short, squat, thick-muscled, I don't walk, but I tromp and swagger. It actually feels quite humorous and, at first, I laugh aloud as I make fists and move my legs.

"What's happening?" asks Ted.

"I'm a big, heavy, dumb guy." I laugh. "My body wants to go THUMP, THUMP, THUMP!"

"Where are you?" he asks.

"I'm that Roman guy. The one I told you about. I see slaves. My slaves. I hate them. I'm a mean son-of-a-bitch!" I feel my forehead wrinkle and my brow become heavy. The anger welling up inside of me is foreign to the woman I am today, but I understand it. I feel blocked and shortsighted, seeing the world only in terms of my own self-interest.

Ted has laid my sketches out in front of him on the coffee table and stares at them. "Victoria, I'm afraid the stress of seeing Barney murdered has created some hallucinations. Or at the very least some hallucinatory dreams."

"Ted, I'm telling you what I feel like when I return to the dream. To the Roman times."

"And it isn't logical," he replies.

"Ted, life isn't logical," I say.

"Maybe not. But it's logical to the logical mind and irrational to the irrational mind," he replies. "And you as a Roman slave owner is irrational."

"Not if you believe in reincarnation," I say.

"I don't."

"Well, I do."

"Okay, Victoria." Ted stands up and walks to the window. Then he turns and looks at me. "I'll tell you what. I'm willing to go with it. Even if the Roman slave owner isn't you, he obviously appeared for a reason."

"Obviously."

"Why don't you lie down, close your eyes and see if you can return to the Roman slave owner? Let's see if he wants to speak to you and me." Ted looks skeptical as he sits in his chair.

I lie back and close my eyes. My first thought is—I need another therapist. My second thought is—there aren't that many to choose from in this town, and at least Ted is willing to look at this. My head begins to pound and I clutch it fearfully.

"Vicky, what's happening?" Ted asks. "Why are you holding your head so tightly?"

I rock back and forth on the sofa, as a creeping pain rises up into my skull. I bang my head on the soft pillows of the couch, but it feels like hard walls. "My head hurts," I cry as tears form in my eyes. "My father, he bashes my head against the wall. He abuses me. He is a powerful and angry man. I cannot resist him."

My father is a gladiator who performs for the pleasure of others; his face beams joyfully over the tortured bodies of his victims. I know this for myself, because I have seen the same expression on his face as he stands over my injured body. My childhood is one of fear and degradation. My entrance into the baths only foreshadows more of the same. I know my father will not protect me from these large, hairy bodies that sit and lounge around the outside of the pool.

"I don't want to see this," I whisper to Ted. I force my mind to turn from the images assaulting it.

"See what?" Ted asks.

"What happens to me."

***

My naked body is stretched out lengthwise across the laps of three men—its pure white, silky flesh contrasting against the hairy, dark legs of my abusers. My genitals tingle with the stimulation, but my mind feels numb and my heart pounds in fear.

"What happens?" he asks.

"They sexually abuse me," I whisper. "One man in particular. A rival of my father's. He wants to control me. To use me to get back at my father, who he hates."

As the years pass, this relationship of sexual slave to master grows more and more heinous, until I feel the child in me die, to be replaced by a hardened, brutalized young man. Any longing for the gentleness of a mother's touch has no place in this world. Now my lips wear the cruel expression of an angry man. A man who whips his slaves for pleasure. My father should be proud, for he has succeeded in making me in his own image. A monster has been created from the frightened child.

"Your father wasn't abusive, Victoria," says Ted.

"Not my father. The Roman boy's father," I say.

"You mean Barney's father was evil," says Ted.

"This isn't Barney's father, Ted. I swear it. This is something else. Someplace else."

Ted is silent. In my mind I see my original dream—the image of the young boy and his mother. Her throat is slashed and she is lying before him. I am a murdering Roman soldier sitting on a horse, staring down at the young boy. I dismount and pick up the child. I hold him in my arms, then place him on the horse, and remount. I will take the boy home and save his life.

The child is beautiful. His face, framed by brown curls, exudes an eager innocence that touches my heart and finds a place there. Some small piece inside of me that remains able to house the emotion of love responds to him joyfully. Over the next ten years as the boy grows to be a handsome young man, I fall deeply in love with him.

***

Ted notices a shaking rise from my body. "Vicky, you're shaking again. What are you feeling?"

I don't want to see what flashes next before my eyes, but it won't be dismissed. "Oh, my God!" I scream. "I murder him! I grew to love him, but then I murdered him!"

The cold blade of the knife glints from my hand. Blood gushes from the limp body lying on the marble floor at my feet. The knife goes in again, and again. The air around me spins and spins, whipping with gale force the exploding rage, mixing it with the bloody viscera.

He did not love me! I cry. He loved my wife. They were making love! He loved her, not me!

I turn to see her standing, frozen in horror, as she witnesses the violent outburst. My body moves slowly toward her; the knife rises above my head ready to gash open her heart. The sight of the uplifted knife jerks her from her panicked stupor and she runs from this madman to save herself. She escapes the fate of the young man.

Blood drips from my hands, but I make no effort to conceal it. I stagger from the room clutching the knife and wander out into streets. People move aside, frightened by the sight of me, a walking corpse seeped in the life-giving liquid of another man. Screams explode from my lungs. The emotions of anger, hatred and love have become mixed into a lethal potion of toxic, bubbling emotional gas, too deadly to be housed inside my body. My screams provide no relief from the churning stew and I plunge the knife into my own organs to relieve the pressure from this evil mixture. The knife searches for the place inside which houses the guilt, and jabs again and again to cut it out of my damaged heart. I loved you! I cry in death. You were the only thing I ever loved, are the last thoughts to penetrate my dying brain before it goes to blackness....

The face of the man I loved and murdered rises before me. I look into his eyes and see that they are Dennis's eyes. "Oh, my God! This boy, this man that I murdered... it is Dennis," I say to Ted. "This is where it all began. I just know it. I murdered him! I loved him. What a horrible, horrible life it was! This is the beginning of our karmic story. I killed him, violently."

There is a long silence.

Ted shakes my shoulder vigorously. "Victoria, come out of it! You are in my office!"

When I open my eyes I see Ted pacing the room, deep in thought. I am only half-aware of him. I am only half in this life. The bloody body still floats before my eyes. My own limbs carry the weight of this ancient guilt.

"It is important to understand the shadow side of the personality," Ted says finally. "I believe that's what you are doing. Projecting your shadow onto this story."

"I'm so drained," I say. "How do I live with this new information?" I moan. "Dear God, how will I ever resolve this?"

Chapter Thirteen

After that session I do my best to erase the horrible feelings that the Roman has woken in me. By Saturday I am feeling much better as my determination to destroy my shadow self once and for all is strengthened. On Saturday night I wriggle my body into a sleek black dress, cut low in front and back, designed to accent my womanly curves, and turn side to side, studying the small abdominal protrusion, wondering if it looks cute and sexy or just fat. I decide it's too small and firm to be fat. I lean over and scrunch my hair, tossing it back as I stand up straight, and poofing it up a bit more to give it maximum fullness. As I lean into the mirror to get a closer look, I imagine the hairy Roman slave owner staring back at me, and I shudder and twitch to shake him off. I am burying him for good, every last bit of him.

My stockings are delicate and they stay up all on their own. Just let him try and slip his big, thick, hairy legs into these! I emit a deep sigh and gratefully step into a pair of high-heeled shoes. Yes indeed, I have successfully erased all signs of the brutal Roman slave owner from my person.

I made reservations at the best restaurant I know; no wagon wheels on the walls, or family-sized portions of meat and potatoes. It's called La Pavilion, and the candles on the tables will erase any signs of imperfection.

I'm taking Gary to dinner with the intention of asking him to marry me. I haven't told anyone, because I know what they would say. WHAT?! ARE YOU CRAZY? But they don't know what I've been going through. The one thing I'm certain of is that I want to put what's in the past behind me and move forward into a better future. Gary is that future.

I also feel I need Gary's wisdom and rational nature desperately right now—but he's still a man, and before I ask him I want to be so ravishingly beautiful and seductive that he can't refuse. I slip a hand in under my breasts and hike them up another inch. Gary loves my breasts. They are his weakness, and my dress shows them off quite advantageously. A little perfume behind the ears, not too much, but just enough so that when he leans in close the aroma will spark his desire. I throw a red woolen wrap over my shoulders and leave it open to expose my all-important cleavage. I didn't tell him where we are going, I only told him to dress nice.

I climb into my little red Toyota and step on the gas, feeling in control for the first time in quite awhile. Gary deserves better than he has been getting, and I vow not to think of anything but him. I'm here and now and that's that. I'm putting the past behind me, praying that the issues with Dennis are dissolved at last, and I can bury them once and for all. My exhaustion after the last regression lasted for two days and now that I'm feeling better I want nothing more than to forget about it.

As I climb out of the car, to escort Gary to dinner properly, I glance down at the fleshy perkiness of my breasts one last time to make sure they catch the light. I lift the heavy lion's head knocker, and let it crash down once, before letting myself inside. Gary comes around the corner as I step into the foyer. He whistles.

"You like?" I reach up and kiss him hard, passionately pressing my body into his. I feel his excitement on my thigh and I get a twinge of pleasure that my outfit is doing what it's supposed to. He grabs my hand to lead me indoors, but I pull away. "Reservations at eight. We don't want to be late."

I'm engineering this entire evening, and I certainly don't want to give away anything too early. As we drive to the restaurant I sense the night tingles with the promise of our union. I turn my head to see him sitting next to me in the car and smile.

"How come you're feeling so happy tonight?" Gary asks. "It's good to see you so upbeat."

"I love you," I say.

"I love you," he says, and leans over to kiss my cheek. "Where are we going?"

"La Pavilion."

"It's not my birthday."

"I know, I wanted to do something special."

We drive on and arrive at the restaurant, but I barely notice, so caught up am I in the script I have written for the evening. Should I ask him before dinner, but after the first glass of wine? Or should I wait until dinner is over? Should I be silly and get on one knee? Or sincere and grab both his hands in mine? Should I act coy and girlish, or take charge and play the role reversal for all it's worth? These questions run over and over in my head until we enter the restaurant and I see candlelight dancing on the tabletops.

The host approaches us. "Reservations?" he asks.

"Yes. Barkley," I say.

He walks over to the book and glances thoughtfully down. "Barkley? There's no Barkley here. Perhaps Madam made them under another name?" He lifts his eyebrows and stares down his long thin nose at me.

"There has to be! Please look again, I made the reservations myself."

"Barkley? I don't remember you making them and I take all the reservations myself."

"Then you are mistaken!" I peer over his shoulder to glance down at the open book. "I made them just yesterday. Two for dinner at eight. Barkley, Victoria. I'm sure I did!"

He tries to block my view, so I push my way past him like a linebacker from the Dallas Cowboys. Jumping from the white pages, scrawled in black ink with sweeping strokes, is the name Octavio Agustus. My heart thumps. My throat catches. Is it possible? Did I imagine it? Somewhere on the other side of my fear is the urge to laugh hysterically at the possibility that I had actually done that. I know I have been thinking a lot about that life, but could I have made the reservations under such a name? I push harder against him to get another glimpse, but he is too strong and he shoves me backward.

"Madame. You did not call yesterday, and even if you had I'm sure I could not have accommodated you at such short notice." He delivers the final thrust to move me away from the book, and gives me a haughty stare. "I do not make mistakes, Ms. Victoria Barkley, but perhaps you do."

"There's no need to be rude!" I yell into his face.

Gary, afraid that we may come to blows, puts his body between us. "Do you have a table for two free anyway?"

"I'm sorry sir, there's nothing this evening." He looks at us coldly, with no sign of compassion.

"There has to be a reservation. This is a special evening!"

"I'm sorry Ma'am. There's nothing to be done." Another couple comes in behind us and he turns his attention away from us and toward them, leaving us standing alone, feeling foolish.

"Come on. We can go somewhere else." Gary takes my hand and leads me out of the restaurant. "Cheer up, it's okay. They are snobs anyway."

"Where should we go?" I feel my breasts sag a couple of inches and my hair go flat.

"I know another place not too far from here."

We climb back in the car, the mood shattered. I wonder, did I actually say Octavio Agustus? Or perhaps, in my distracted state, I never made those reservations at all. I can't bring myself to fully admit it. "Jerks," I say under my breath.

"Let it go," Gary says. "It'll be okay. We can have fun anyway." He strokes my leg to comfort me. "You want me to drive?"

"Okay." I climb back out of the car and sit in the passenger seat as Gary climbs in behind the wheel. We drive for fifteen minutes and pull into the parking lot of The Bird and the Beast. If La Pavilion is three stars, it's a half. "How's this?" Gary asks.

"Okay," I lie.

We enter and I shrug a half-hearted acceptance. Even if there are no wagon wheels it does a pretty poor job of mimicking a New England Inn. In the fireplace I notice red lights dancing behind plastic logs. I remove my coat and my breasts catch the eyes of every red-blooded heterosexual man in the place. The lights are not dim enough to hide my blushing cheeks.

Gary ushers me to a table and I glance around to see that it appears to be a local dating spot for the high school and college crowd. "I need a drink," I say. "Where's a waitress?"

A smiling twenty-one year old girl dressed as an English wench, complete with white puffy hat and frilly apron, comes to the table. "How are you this evening?" she asks perkily.

"Fine," Gary answers. I sulk.

"Can I help you?" she asks.

"I'll have a vodka martini. Two olives," I say.

"I'll have the same," Gary says.

A loud laugh pierces the room as a fraternity boy, drinking heavily from the look of it, slaps his buddy on the arm.

"Double dating," I whisper to Gary. "And drunk. Boy, he'll impress her tonight."

"I think she's as drunk as he is," Gary says. "Look at the two overturned bottles of champagne sitting next to the table. The two girls probably finished those off."

I open the menu and see chicken, fish and steak. "Salads are probably made with iceberg lettuce. I was all set for endive. It's my fault. I probably forgot to call."

"It's okay. Let's forget about it and enjoy ourselves."

The waitress puts the martinis down on the table. "Ready to order?"

"No. Come back." Another loud laugh assaults my eardrums. I take a large gulp from the martini. Pull yourself together, Vicky. This is supposed to be your night to make Gary happy. I smile at him and reach over and stroke his cheek. "What are you having?"

"Pasta. You?"

"I don't know."

I signal the waitress. "Can we have another round?"

"Sure," she says. "Are you almost ready to order?"

"After the drinks," I reply. I reach my hand over to Gary. I'm beginning to think I'd better go with the sweet and sincere approach. I chew on my olives as the next round of drinks is brought to the table.

"To you." I raise my glass to Gary. He returns the gesture and we both take a large sip. "Gary?" The martinis have taken hold.

"Yes?"

"Nothing." I take another large sip of my drink and spill a little bit on my chin. I glance guiltily over at the college girls falling all over their dates. I'd better slow down or I'll end up like them—a drunk woozy, floozy making an idiot of myself.

A loud scream emerges from the drunken college student's table. A roll gets winged from one fraternity jock to the head of the other. His girlfriend whacks him on the arm. Another roll comes back at them. The other girl falls sideways out of her seat and is caught, just in time, by her boyfriend, who pulls her upright.

"Gary?"

"What is it?" he looks amused. "You better slow down with that second martini."

"Gary," I pick the olive out of the glass, suddenly too drunk to care about the form of the presentation, "Gary, will you marry me?" I whisper my proposal at the exact moment that the drunken co-ed stands up from her chair, leans into the champagne bucket, and vomits repeatedly into it. "BLAACCCH!!!" comes retching out of her mouth, just as the words are leaving mine.

"What?" Gary says as we both turn our heads to see her dinner fly out of her mouth.

I put my face in my hands, lay my head on the table and groan as all hell breaks loose in the restaurant. I can't move. From the depths of my despair I hear Gary begin to laugh. First quietly to himself, and then louder and louder until he can't contain himself. Waitresses rush around, grabbing towels. Customers recoil in horror. The world is coming apart around me. Cries of "Let's get out of here" and "That's disgusting" assault my eardrums. A loud crash signals the overturning of the champagne bucket full of puke. The poor girl can't seem to stop vomiting and Gary can't stop laughing like a madman at the absurdity of the situation.

"No, Vicky," he says between howls of laughter. "I won't marry you." I lift my head and watch him.

"Why?" I ask as another round of vomit leaves the fleeing co-ed.

He grabs my hand and lifts me up out of my seat. "Let's get the hell out of here!" He drags me to the coat check and out the door without pausing to pay for the martinis. When we get in the car he is still laughing. I am not amused.

"Why won't you marry me?"

"Don't be absurd! Let's not do this now."

"I want to do it now. I'm ready to get married and I love you."

"When we get married I want it to be right, not a reaction on your part."

"It's not a reaction!"

He raises his eyebrows to make his point.

"It isn't. I love you. I do."

"I know you love me. And I love you, but let's talk about this later. Let's be sure, and not decide this with the sounds of vomit in our ears."

I hunch down in my seat. "This is the worst night of my life. Take me home."

"Vick," he pleads.

"Just take me home, please. I have a headache," I say. I've never felt so stupid and vulnerable in all my life." Gary drives me home in silence.

"I'll bring the car back tomorrow morning," he says as he lets me off.

"Whatever." I exit the car without even looking at him.

Chapter Fourteen

A rotund woman in a flowered housecoat steps out of the sorority with a broom in her hands to sweep the door-step. I haven't seen Mrs. Thompson since the shooting. My guess is she was asked to resign and left town, or maybe she's rotting in jail as an accomplice. This new "mother" is older, but her face is friendlier than Mrs. Thompson's. I think about going out-side to introduce myself but decide against it. I step back from the window as the phone rings.

"I want to apologize for laughing at you last night. I wasn't laughing at the proposal of marriage, I swear it," Gary says before I even say hello.

"It's okay." The tone of my voice doesn't match the easy for-giveness.

"Really. Come to the café so we can talk."

"Okay." I pick up Cleopatra. She purrs into the phone.

"I mean it, Vick. I'm really sorry."

"I know. I'll see you later." I hang up. I'm going to make him suffer a little before I accept his apology. But I plan to make-up with him—I understand why he laughed at my proposal. The truth is, it isn't really Gary I'm angry at. It's life. It's death. It's Ted, my dumb-ass therapist, I'm angry at. It's Barney's father I'm angry at. It's that stupid, murdering Roman I'm angry at. The truth is, Gary is way down the list when it comes to what is making me angry right now.

I vow that I will never see Dennis again—at least not on pur-pose. Every time I think of him I feel sick to my stomach. I'll ask

Gary, Sally and her new boyfriend Michael over for dinner to-night. Gary and I will be back to old times and we can forget the whole nasty incident of last night.

I call Gary back up. "Hey, honey. Why don't you come over for dinner tonight? I'll ask Sally and Michael and we'll have a cozy Sunday night."

"Sounds great. Vick?"

"Yeah?"

"Thanks for forgiving me," Gary says quietly.

"Just don't do it again," I say.

"I promise," he replies.

At six o'clock I light a fire in the fireplace and put out a bottle of red wine. I plan to serve garlic bread, salad and spaghetti primavera. During dinner everyone is very careful not to mention Barney's death.

After dinner Michael supplies a joint. It's been years since I smoked and after two hits I stand up and dance solo to the oldies coming from the radio.

Sally is happy with Michael; they've gone into the snugly phase which sometimes annoys me but tonight makes me happy for her. I twirl and swirl around the room, glad to be alive for the first time in awhile. I know Gary is watching me and that makes me happy too. He has beautiful eyes, very doe-like, and right now I am per-fectly contented to feel them focused on me.

I take another hit of the joint and tell myself that life is really good after all. I mean, look at Gary—he's the greatest, I think. I have a good job, a nice house and good friends. I smile and twirl. I also have strange visions that I don't really understand and a therapist who thinks I'm wigging out. My twirling slows down. I just witnessed the death of a favorite student, shot by his own father. I stop twirling and sway from leg to leg. Dennis thinks I'm nuts and so does Tom. And I'm facing a student production of *Hamlet*, which has to be cast soon. I stop swaying and stand still and stare at Gary. I see Gary staring at me. He's frowning.

"Life sucks," I say. "Life really, really sucks." I collapse onto the sofa next to him and bury my face in his chest.

Gary stretches out his hand and touches my back gently. "I know it's been hard, Victoria. But you'll pull through."

"This time I really mean it—life really, really, really sucks. Can I have more wine?" I reach for my glass and offer it up to Gary for a refill. He refills it. Sally and Michael are staring at me. "Sorry guys," I say to them. "Go on with your snuggling, don't let my morose nature interfere with your first-stage romantic idealism." Sally sticks her tongue out at me. "Gary, tell me a story. Please," I beg.

"A story?" he asks. "Like what?"

"A good story. A happy story."

"A happy story? Oh, you mean a fairy tale."

"Right, nothing real. Just happy."

"Once upon a time—" he begins.

"Yeah, once upon a time a beautiful princess and a handsome prince, and a castle and lots of thorns to cut through, and then a wicked witch, who gets her head cut off, and lots of kissing at the end," I say.

"Maybe you should tell me the story," he says.

"All my stories are sad ones. Everyone gets murdered and haunts the castle walls and drives everyone else mad and then the lovers never get together and do the most horrendous things to each other and are doomed to live eternally in a state of agony and unfulfilled longing."

"Pretty dark stuff," he says. "Look at Sally and Michael over there. Do they look tortured and unfulfilled?"

"No, just naïve."

Sally interrupts us. "You guys want to go to a movie?"

I look at Gary, who shrugs his shoulders. "What movie?"

We decide on a foreign film, something French. I am expecting one of those films where the man is obsessed with the ankles of every woman under the age of eighteen. We bundle up and step out into the cold air. On the way to the movie, kept warm in the back seat of Sally's car by Gary's embrace, I can almost imagine that everything is going to be okay again. There isn't a line when we get to the theater and we rush in and easily find a seat seconds before the lights come down on us.

"You want something?" I whisper to Gary. "I'm really thirsty and I need a coke."

"I'll share yours if that's okay. Get a large one."

"Okay." I sneak my way out of the darkened theater.

It seems almost impossible, but it happens. Standing at the counter, getting two boxes of popcorn is Dennis. I think of running away to West Texas as fast as I can. We haven't seen each other since the bar when I poured my heart out to him and he ran away, came back and kissed me, and then left again, leaving me feeling like an idiot. Now here he is getting popcorn for himself and wifey-poo.

"Hey Dennis, what's up?"

"Hey, Vicky." He smiles innocently.

This really enrages me. I pour my heart out to him, he kisses me, and now he pretends that nothing happened! "I think we need to talk," I say.

He pulls away. Shields up full force. Impenetrable. "Now?"

"Yeah. Outside." He definitely does not want to be here with me, does not want to have this conversation, and has the belief that all this would be much better resolved by pretending nothing ever happened. He follows me outside.

"What's up?" he asks.

"What do you think is up?" He makes me feel insane, as if all this is my imagination working overtime and he and I have never met before. He is cold to me. I have forgotten what drama it is we are re-enacting and I don't care. I am angry and hurt and rejected. He succeeds brilliantly in creating in me the appropriate feelings.

"Revenge is sweet," the Roman boy whispers in Octavio Agustus's ear.

The cold air hits my face but I don't care, I am going to have it out with him here and now.

"Listen, Vicky," he says. "You have got to stop this. It's not any good, this past life stuff. Even if what you say is true, it's in the past. Let it go. It's today now." He speaks to me in a placating fashion, like a sensible old man to his five-year-old grandchild.

I look in his eyes and they give him away. There is nothing neutral in those eyes. He wants to pretend he is neutral and I am the raving maniac, but his eyes don't lie.

"I see. This is all me. Is that what you are saying?"

"I've got a wife and a child and another one on the way and I'm trying to respect that fact," Dennis says.

"Well you are doing a real bad job of it and doing a wonderful job of pretending that you are doing a good job of it," I yell at him.

"It doesn't matter what I want or what you want. Whatever feelings I had for you when we first met have no place in my life," he says.

His answer echoes in my brain. My God, I think, he is becoming Jean and I am becoming Franklin and we can't stop ourselves even when we are made aware of what we are doing. We are being drawn by something more powerful than us to do this—to reverse roles and act out this tragedy as though it were some Shakespearean drama.

I really hate him right now. His pseudo-neutral gaze, his attempt at rationality. His denial of the fantasies he's had of us making love. The denial of his own feelings.

"Damn you," I say. "Don't you get it?"

His eyes look sad. It is his only concession to his feelings. It is all it takes for me to love him again. It takes so very little for me to believe that he will give in, will allow himself the full expression of his soul.

"I've got to get inside. Rebecca is going to wonder where I am. This popcorn is going to be cold."

"Good. I hope she asks you why and you tell her the truth," I say. He doesn't answer, but turns away and runs inside, leaving me, once again, in the cold.

I have no where to go. I can't go in and sit through the movie. I can't stay outside and freeze to death. I go inside and sit in the lobby shivering. I am sure that he has convinced himself that I am some amoral whore and he is pure morality; I am woman of darkness ready to lead him away from his woman of light. This thought of him judging me makes me insane. I feel like I could explode and take him with me. I have no objectivity, and the thought of this being pure karmic retribution has left me. All I can do is feel. I am consumed by these feelings. I think of Ted and his talk of the shadow side. How he told me that each of us has a shadow and we must bring it to the light. I feel like Dennis is dumping his shadow onto me and asking me to take responsibility for both of us. I don't want to carry his shadow for him. I want him to share equally in this creation.

Gary comes out of the theater looking for me. I've been gone fifteen minutes, at least.

"What's the matter?" He sits next to me on the window ledge.

"He's here. Dennis is here." Gary knows who I'm talking about.

"What happened?"

I pause and take in a deep breath. "Nothing. Let's watch the movie."

Chapter Fifteen

Our plane lands at the Newark airport at 12:51 p.m. If Gary is nervous about meeting my parents for the first time he doesn't show it, except for a slight stiffening when he walks down the long ramp toward the gate.

"There she is!" I wave to my mother standing apart from the throng of well-wishers. Her stiffly coifed blonde hair and elegant stature separate her from the crowd. "Victoria!" she calls with delight.

"Hey, Mom." I rush to give her a kiss on the cheek. "Mom, I'd like you to meet Gary Dubitsky. Gary, my Mom." They shake hands with polite awkwardness.

"Nice to meet you Gary."

"Nice to meet you, Mrs. Barkley."

"Please, call me Sondra. I couldn't bear to hear Mrs. Barkley for four days!"

Gary's shoulders visibly relax and he says, "Sondra it is."

The drive from the airport to the upper east side of Manhattan takes twice as long as usual in the rush of Thanksgiving traffic. My mother's curiosity about Gary has plenty of time to be satisfied. In fact, in the two hours it takes before we arrive at 88th and Park she manages to extract his life story. Even I never knew that he was born a week overdue and weighed ten and a half pounds.

I greet our doorman, Harry, with a smile and a kiss on the cheek. "Uncle Harry," I address him with the nickname I gave him as a child, "I'd like you to meet Gary Dubitsky. My boyfriend."

"A pleasure to meet you, Gary Dubitsky," Harry says and winks in my direction. "Here, let me help you with those bags." He loads them into the elevator.

Thanksgiving dinner begins with Dad standing at the end of the table, the carving fork and knife held firmly in his hands. His temples are lightly gray, and his belt only slightly pushed out by age. At fifty-nine he's thinking of early retirement—too much time in corporate law. Part of him still yearns for his early and idealistic years in trial law as an Assistant District Attorney.

"Who wants dark meat?" he asks as he cuts the legs from the large bird. He waves the fork at our guests, the Baldwins, to extract requests. The Baldwins are strangers to me. Mother invited them because they recently moved in across the hall. Mrs. Baldwin nods her lacquered hair in a polite yes. Her two sons hold out their plates and bob their heads up and down quickly. Mr. Baldwin doesn't move a muscle.

"No turkey for me," Gary says, "I've pretty much given up on all meat and poultry."

"Me neither, Dad."

"What!" Mom says. "Why didn't you tell me? I go and buy this enormous bird. Come on, Victoria, you've got to eat." Her eyes implore me.

"Okay. A little white meat for me."

"How about you Gary?"

"None for me, thanks. It looks delicious, but there is plenty of wonderful-looking food to eat," he says. He throws her a charming smile and she backs down. Plates are passed, the Baldwins are served, and Mom is happy again once Mr. Baldwin requests extra white meat and gravy.

I begin eating the minute everyone's plate is full, which is common practice at my house. To my left, my ears detect a slight throat clearing sound emanating from petite Mrs. Baldwin. Something about that sound draws my attention away from my mouthful of sinfully delicious apple, walnut, sweet potatoes in brandy and brown sugar sauce. My special recipe. I peer up from the plate to see

Gary, Mom and Dad eating, but the Baldwins sitting stock still at their plates.

"I think perhaps the Baldwins would like to say grace," I say.

"If you don't mind," Mrs. Baldwin says in her crisp voice.

"Of course not," my mother says.

My father puts down his fork and patiently sits chewing a piece of turkey he has popped in his mouth.

We all bow our heads while Mrs. Baldwin mumbles, barely audible, something about God and food and eternal something or another. My father looks relieved when the mumbling stops and immediately digs into a large mound of mashed potatoes swimming in gravy.

"Amen," say the Baldwins in chorus.

"Amen," says my father, his mouth full of food.

This should be a real joy, I think. "So Dad?" I say cheerfully. "What's up with you these days?"

"Actually I'm off to Japan on business. I'm getting to hate that trip. It really knocks it out of me."

"I never went to Japan. It's one of the few places I never visited," Gary says.

"You traveled a bit?" Dad asks.

"Oh yes. For about eight years after high school. Mostly around Europe. Backpacked and worked when I could find a job. I never got to Japan, but I always wanted to. I feel drawn to it and would like to visit someday."

"You traveled around Europe for eight years?" Mrs. Baldwin asks with an astonished look on her face. "Wasn't that dangerous?"

"I never thought about it as dangerous," Gary says. "I mean I wasn't selling drugs in Turkey or anything."

Mrs. Baldwin doesn't laugh. "I should hope not." The kids, I judge to be about nine and ten, smirk at each other.

"Actually, Europe is quite a bit safer than the United States in many ways. Traveling is easier, the trains are excellent for the most part, and many people are tourists. I loved Amsterdam."

I can see where this is leading. Mrs. Baldwin has pushed one of his rare buttons and he is determined to rile her to the max. It max. It shouldn't be hard. "In Amsterdam you can buy hash cakes in the bars," he continues. "It's legal there, you know."

Mrs. Baldwin turns white and the kids snicker. I don't know what possesses her, but then my mother says, "I always wanted to make those Alice B. Toklas brownies. You know, the ones with marijuana in them."

Gary howls with laughter. Mrs. Baldwin clamps down and begins shoveling the food into her mouth. Mr. Baldwin appears to have been absent from this entire interchange. I would guess he lives most of his life somewhere else when he is at home. The kids seem to be enjoying the way the conversation is going.

"Well, I don't know about Amsterdam and hash cakes," Dad says, "but I do enjoy some of the pleasures of Tokyo."

I guess we won't be seeing the Baldwins again.

"What are you up to these days, Victoria?" Dad asks. "How is teaching?"

"Okay. My favorite class is one on *Romeo and Juliet*. First we study Shakespeare, then we study comparative literature from other cultures. Love and tragedy appeals to the college spirit—and mine too."

"They say that Romeo and Juliet were only fourteen years of age when they fell in love," Gary says.

I've never seen him so eager to get under somebody's skin, but obviously Mrs. Baldwin brings it out in him.

"That's about right. Teenagers can fall in love as strongly and passionately as adults."

"I sure did," Gary says. "There's nothing like the first time."

Holy shit! Is he going to start in on teenagers having sex? Mrs. Baldwin will just pass out, but first she will clamp her hands over the kids' ears. They are obviously not native New Yorkers and unused to the constant assault of sexual references in advertising and theater notices that daily greet the residents of this fine town.

Thankfully, no one says anything for a few minutes as the only sounds are chewing and shoveling. Dad pours more wine for everyone, except poor Mrs. Baldwin, who drinks soda.

Suddenly, out of nowhere, Gary says, "So Sondra. What do you think of reincarnation? You a believer?"

The color drains from my face. Religion is kind of a no-no in my household. Far worse than sex and drugs as a topic of conversation.

"Reincarnation? Why?" my mother asks.

"Vicky has been doing some research on the subject."

I want to kill him. I glare at him, but he doesn't seem to notice. He must be too busy thinking of what else he can say to rile our guests.

"Vicky?" Dad says. "Why?"

"Just interested."

"Makes sense to me," says Gary.

"Not to me," Mom says. "Stupid." She doesn't elaborate.

"Never thought much about it," Dad says.

"What purpose is there to reincarnation?" Mrs. Baldwin asks. "The purpose of life is to live it as Jesus did and then go to heaven when you die."

"Then I'm doomed," Dad says, rather nastily. "I've never even been crucified."

Gary laughs.

"Don't be so sure," I say, surprising myself with the reply. "Maybe in another life you were." I glance over to see Mrs. Baldwin's jaw hang open, a piece of stuffing protruding from her mouth.

"That is a sin!" Mrs. Baldwin yells.

The boy to her right slides his hand over toward his Dad's wineglass and takes a sip without his Dad even noticing. This has got to be a nightmare, I hope.

"A sin?" I ask Mrs. Baldwin. "I don't think I'm a sinner."

"God will be the judge of that!" she says. "I think we had better be going." She grabs the kids, one in each hand, and lifts them from the table. Mr. Baldwin looks at her and blinks. "Come on, Edgar." He rises from the table and follows her. The door slams behind them before we speak again.

"Holy shit! Mom? Why did you invite them?"

"Did you have to bring up reincarnation?" she says to me.

"I didn't," I say glaring at Gary.

"Why on earth are you thinking about reincarnation?" she continues.

"Sorry, Vicky," Gary says.

"Vicky, are you doing something weird?" Dad says.

"Weird? Weird? What the hell is that supposed to mean?" I push myself away from the table. "Excuse me, I have to go to the bathroom."

I sit on the toilet and put my face in my hands. I've got to get out of here. My father does crossword puzzles when he sits on the john, and I reach for a pencil and a scrap piece of paper and write a note. *Gone out, be back shortly. Vicky.* I leave the note on the table in the hallway on my way out.

As I emerge from the apartment building, I notice the ground is cast with long shadows from the fading November sun. Glancing up toward the sky I see streaks of pink melting into the gray blue, and long, thin wisps of far off cirrus clouds. Thanksgiving traffic is minimal, and an unusual quiet hangs over Park Avenue at almost four o'clock on a Thursday afternoon. I head west toward Central Park, determined to leave my family behind and find some place where I can be at peace with my thoughts. I enter the park and walk by the Metropolitan Museum of Art, remembering the times I ditched high school and went there to roam the halls. Sometimes my girlfriend, Judy, would go with me and we would visit the Egyptian wing and imagine that we were alive in the age of the Pharaohs. Judy was convinced she had been a High Priestess of great importance, but I was always sure that it was more likely we would have been slaves or something. "Who do you think built all those pyramids?" I used to ask her. She never wanted to think about that part.

The park is scattered with people walking off their turkey dinners, and an occasional jogger or rollerblader, who probably only consumed sensible amounts of food and immediately donned their exercise gear and went to burn it off. A group of sweat-shirted, dirty males, clutching a football, brush past after their pre-dinner game I would guess. I don't think they ate dinner and then threw themselves around in the dirt; probably late eaters and the wives are all at home cooking.

I am aimless. I wonder what they will say back at home when they realize that I ducked out. I only feel slightly guilty for leaving Gary. He certainly didn't come to my rescue. God, I feel alone right now. I walk further into the park and sit myself on a bench to watch the pigeons. A snack cart entices me over to buy a pretzel with the money in my pocket. I figure I might as well feed the birds.

As I approach the cart, an elderly man standing about twenty feet away on the other side stares at me intently. His ragged, brown tweed jacket is held together by a single button, and his throat is warmed by a thick, red woolen scarf, wound over and over about his neck. Feeling uneasy, I don't look at him, but walk directly up to the hot dog seller and ask for a pretzel.

I grab the pretzel and go back to my bench, hoping that I was wrong about the man, and that he wasn't really staring at me but merely enjoying an afternoon in the park. I glance around and see that there are still a few people drifting here and there, so I figure I'm okay even if his intentions are not entirely honorable.

"Here pidgey, pidgey," I call and break off a piece of pretzel to attract their attention. Three pigeons swoop down on me and eagerly scoop up the crumbs.

"Hungry little guys, aren't they?" he says.

I cautiously lift my head to see the man standing about four feet away from me. How did he sneak up on me?

"I guess so," I say coldly, averting my eyes to indicate I have no desire to talk.

"I bring my own bread," he says and sits down right next to me on the bench and pulls out a loaf of stale french bread from a brown paper bag. I notice his fingers are reddened slightly from the cold air.

I prepare to scooch my body aside and walk away. I lived in New York City long enough to immediately return to my old defenses, and take the position of assuming the worst of my fellow man—always look for those concealed weapons, my subway training tells me. I am certain that any moment I will recognize the stench of a homeless person. A smell so sour that it can repel even the softest hearted among humans, but instead I notice a sweet

I notice a sweet smell drift past my nose, reminding me of jasmine. It causes me to glance in his direction, and as I do he turns his head toward me. His eyes contain a silent but peaceful mystery that says "I am known to you," but they aren't frightening, and they don't make me want to run away. They are calm, grounded eyes—eyes that encourage me to speak. "You feed the birds often?" I ask.

"Almost everyday. Especially in winter. Squirrels too, of course. Central Park provides lots of crumbs year around, but it doesn't hurt to give them something extra in the cold months." He smiles and extends his hand. "My name's Hawkins. What's yours?"

I hesitate, wondering why I'm talking to him. I should probably leave, but for some reason I don't; instead I cautiously take his hand and say, "I am Victoria."

"Families can sure be a pain on holidays, can't they?" he says suddenly.

"Yeah. Is yours a pain?"

"My family is long gone. But yours isn't, and I gathered you came here to get some breathing room from them." I turn back to face him and allow myself to study his features. He appears to be about sixty, neither old nor young. His face is not easily categorized, but mostly I guessed he was a mixture of Asian and African-American, with exotic eyes and a full flat nose and round smiling lips. His silky, straight dark hair hangs in wisps about his head, and just brushes the edge of the scarf he has wrapped about his neck. "Ha! I got you there!"

I laugh and smile and relax. "Yep, Hawkins. You got me there."

"So what they troubling you about?"

"Everything."

"Families got that down good. They know exactly how to make us confront what we don't want to look at. And they never seem to do it without maximum irritation." He pops the next crumb of bread into his own mouth, disappointing the waiting birds. "What did you fight about?"

"Reincarnation," I reply, surprising myself by my lack of caution.

"Ah, well… reincarnation…" he muses. "Don't be saddened. What you lose comes back around. It merely changes form. The baby weaned from mother's milk now drinks sweet wine. God's joy moves from box to box, from atom to atom. As rain moves into the flowerbed. As flowers, up from the ground. Now it looks like a plate of rice. Now a mountain cloaked in clouds. Now a horse being tamed. It hides within these things 'til one day it bursts them open…"

"That's Rumi!" I say in delight. "Isn't it? Isn't it Rumi?"

"Inspired by him, certainly."

"How do you know Rumi?"

"Hmmm, thirteenth century, if my mind serves me correctly."

"Thirteenth century Persia?"

"Yep. I was a Sufi. The way I look at life, we've all done our time as plants, animals and humans. We've even been a cloud. At some point the soul learns all it can about life on Earth and doesn't return. Except in rare cases, of course, like when we incarnate briefly to help another soul."

My mouth hangs open and my hands freeze in mid-air. He looks at me and laughs—a loud, hearty belly-laugh. "Ha! I got you again didn't I, Miss Victoria?"

A smile breaks over my astonished face and I find my heart lightening with a joy I had long forgotten. "You got me again, Hawkins. You got me again you rascal!"

"Rascal. I like being called a rascal. It has a bit of whimsy in it."

A pigeon flashes its wings and flies upward to land on his head. He doesn't brush it off, but turns his head slowly in my direction to model his newest attire. "How do I look?"

"Every bit the picture of *haute couture*. That's unless it decides to take a poop!"

Hawkins rises from the bench, and as he walks slowly away, the pigeons at his feet join in beside him forming a small parade. The pigeon hat sits happily atop his silky hair, bobbing up and down with each step.

"Hey, wait up!" I call after him and rush to his side, scaring the nesting pigeon that lifts, startled, into the air.

"The fashion world is so fickle," says Hawkins as he touches his bare head.

For a few minutes we walk, side-by-side, in peaceful silence. A strange urge overtakes me. I want to hold his hand. To feel like a child again, clutching the safe and secure hand of a parent guided along without having to question the destination. As this thought arises inside of me, Hawkins stops and turns to face me. "You aren't alone, Miss Victoria. Not at all. If you could see all the angels and guides that surround you right now, you'd never feel alone again. Close your eyes and feel with your heart. Your heart knows that you are never alone."

The understanding I've been looking for in friends and family, I've found here with this man I know only as Hawkins. It's not in what he says, but something much more intangible—I feel he knows my heart better than anyone else. Tears well up in my eyes and I throw my arms around him and let them fall down my cheeks onto his chest. As my face pushes into the body of this stranger, I notice again the sweet smell of jasmine filling my head with its aroma. "I'm sorry." I sniffle and pull away. "I can't imagine what made me do that."

He pulls a clean, pressed, white hanky from his pocket and offers it to me. "It's all part of the path back to God, you know," he says as he strokes my cheek gently with his rough finger and wipes away a teardrop. "It doesn't make it any easier when you are in the middle of it, I suppose, but from the perspective of up there," he points at the sky, "it's just an eyeblink. A glorious eyeblink, none-the-less. No soul is lost forever in the maze of lives. Every soul has many, many lives, but every soul returns to God. All paths lead back to God. That's very hard for humans to understand. Everyone wants to think that their path is the only path, but all paths are leading back to God."

"Some take longer, I guess."

"Don't be quick to judge which path is longer..." he says. "I danced on the edge of madness, wanting to know why. I pounded on the door. It opened. I was pounding from the inside."

"Rumi again?"

"I was having a bad day that day, as I recall. He was trying to help," he says and moves his hands, making them dance up toward the sky and down to the earth. "Ha!" He laughs again and skips away from me toward the open grassy field. Suddenly he flings his body, head over feet, into a wild somersault. He springs up again, landing on his feet and repeats the roll, again and again. "Come on, Victoria. It feels wonderful!"

I race after him, and with abandon, throw myself over and over in a series of cartwheels and spins. Hawkins stands back and watches me, then his hands come together and he begins to clap and stomp his feet in rhythm. Clomp, clomp, stomp, clap, he reels about in utter joy, making music with his body. His mouth opens and a joyous hoot emerges as he accompanies himself in this one-man jamboree. Soon I join him, and like two chimpanzees we cavort in the cold, fading November light. We race about hooting and clapping until I fall to the ground exhausted, my chest heaving to catch my breath. Hawkins stands over me, his breath drawing into his chest in easy rhythms, as though he hadn't moved an inch.

"Aren't you exhausted, Mr. Hawkins?" I gasp. "I feel so good!" I shout. "Tired but really, really, really good!"

"That, my dear Victoria, is how the angels dance." He lays his body on the ground next to me and we stare into the darkening sky. "It's marvelous to look at."

"Even in New York City?"

"Even in New York City. The age of conquering is slowly drawing to a close, you know. Conquering the Earth, HA, as if such a thing were possible. Conquering one another, HA, as if such a thing were possible. Conquering the animals and the insects, even the heavens, HA, as if such a thing were possible!"

"It's drawing to a close?" I ask.

"Not in your lifetime, of course. Well not in this lifetime I should say. But in some lifetime, you will know, a time when man lives peacefully on the Earth."

"Not as long as Donald Trump is building more and more casinos," I say sarcastically.

"Humans must learn to conquer, before they can learn to let go," he says softly. "It's how you are made."

"We are made?" I ask. "Not you?"

"Oh I did plenty of conquering in my time. I was even a fierce plundering, murdering Hun in one lifetime. Spent a bit of time cleaning up the karma from that life!" He laughs.

"Are you an angel now, Hawkins?"

"An angel? Oh my, do you think I'm an angel? Then I guess I am. How many angels can fit on the head of a pin? As many as you want to be there!" He rises from the damp earth and reaches out his hand to lift me off.

We stand, face to face, as he strokes my cheek. "Don't be afraid, dear Victoria, you are on your path. Close your eyes and feel the love that surrounds you."

I close my eyes and imagine angels all around, their wings touching my shoulders and their harps singing songs of joy and peace. "Hawkins?" I say, my eyes still closed. "Hawkins, I love you." I open my eyes, and reach out my hand to touch his, but I am alone. "Hawkins? Where are you? Hawkins?" I walk onto the path to look for him. "Hawkins? Where did you go?"

In the darkening light, a retreating form skips lightly away. "Is that him?" I wonder. "How did he get so far away in such a short time?" The wind blows through the trees, and from a distant dream I hear him say, "I love you too, Victoria," and he is gone.

When I return to the apartment, I am no longer angry with my family and my boyfriend. I walk into the study where they are gathered around the television, and Gary rises to greet me.

"Where did you go, Victoria? I was starting to worry about you," he says.

"I went to talk to the angels." I whisper in his ear, and hold him close to me until the warmth of his chest radiates into mine.

Chapter Sixteen

The Café Bacchanal is under siege by the Dunkin' Donuts across the street and a new Starbucks two blocks away. Gary says he's not worried, but I know he is. Even in the cold, the construction goes on and it looks like the Starbucks will be ready to go by January. They took over an old five and dime while we were in NYC and put up a large sign on posts in front of it that reads FUTURE HOME OF STARBUCKS. The town board must have approved the plan quickly; Gary hadn't heard a thing.

Today Gary's café is packed with students, and there isn't a calm one among them. The large smoking section is overflowing into the non-smoking section but nobody seems to mind. Books are opened at every table and arguments erupt here and there over a chemistry formula or Jackson Pollack's influence on abstract art. Finals are next week.

I'm drinking a large cappuccino and staring at my sketches Gary thumb-tacked onto the walls. Because they don't contain any familiar faces, the students ignore them. The sketch of Jean running down cobblestone streets in the rain, with a carriage disappearing around a corner in front of her, makes me very uncomfortable. I don't know why I agreed to let him put them up. The sketches of the Roman life are tucked under my bed at home. I haven't told Gary about that life, and I don't plan to.

The front door opens and a tall, thin blond woman enters the café. She is wearing cowboy boots, Levis, a hand knit sweater and she carries a briefcase. Although incongruous, the look works.

At least for her. She immediately walks to the counter. "Hey, Gary," she says. He turns and smiles.

Wait a minute. I've never seen her in here before. How come she knows Gary so well? I lean toward them and strain over the noise to hear.

"Linda, it's great to see you." Gary walks over to her and gives her a kiss on the cheek. "How you been?"

"Good but tired. If I survive my Ph.D. it will be a miracle. I'm back in town and settled here for awhile. The research is done and now I have to write, write, write."

Ph.D.? Damn!

"What you want?" asks Gary.

"A double espresso and a big gooey slice of cake." She points to the chocolate double layered cake in the glass display case. "I probably shouldn't, it will make me fat, but…."

"Fat?" Gary interrupts. "I don't think you have to worry about that!" He extracts the cake from the case and puts in on the counter. Then he cuts a huge slice. Almost twice the size of a normal piece.

"Gary, that's huge," says Linda.

"Enjoy," he replies.

She runs her index finger through the fudge icing and licks it off. For a moment I almost think she's going to put her finger in his mouth.

"Have a seat," says Gary. "I'll bring your espresso over to you."

"Thanks," she replies. She picks up her briefcase in one hand, puts the cake plate in the other, and walks to an empty chair.

Sitting near her, their chairs drawn close together, are a young couple. His left hand entwines around her right. Two open books lie on the table before them, but they go unnoticed. The boy leans over and kisses her, pressing his lips so hard onto hers that the kiss draws breath from my chest. I am reminded of a photograph I saw of a movie star sitting with his girlfriend smooching in an outdoor café I remember thinking how pure and succulent their love seemed. How easily I fell into the image—one moment in time captured on a one-dimensional surface—representing for millions of people the unattainable, gorgeous, sexy, vision of our collective fantasies.

That fantasy has changed forever for me. There will never again be "one moment in time," but only many, many moments strung endlessly together weaving the brilliant tapestry of a soul. No longer will lovers exist separate and untouched by the pull of time and consequence.

I turn away from the lovers and look again at the sketch tacked to the wall of Jean running helplessly after Franklin. Gary walks by carrying Linda's espresso and sits down in the chair across from her. She perches on the edge of her seat and smiles at him with a look that reveals far more than a mere cup of coffee warrants.

I now understand what people mean when they say, "My heart dropped into my stomach." That's what it feels like. Watching Gary talking with Linda makes me feel ill. Has he slept with her? Is that possible? Maybe not now, but maybe before he and I were together. She said she'd been away. Maybe it was earlier, two or three years before.

I take a last sip of cappuccino, slip my arms into my jacket, pick up my briefcase and leave the café. I can't stand to be in the same room with them. Gary doesn't notice my exit.

It's threatening snow, but nothing comes. The sun is almost below the horizon and the sky is cloudy except for a streak of purple-blue in the west. I zip up my jacket and head for home.

As my class on *Romeo and Juliet* wraps up this semester I turn my attention to *Hamlet*. Second semester will begin with the arduous task of directing the play but first semester ends with casting it. The next day, I'm sitting in the darkened theater, waiting for the next auditioner to read. This one has chosen the *To be or not to be* speech, and his childish voice, attempting to be both noble and profound, is lulling me with these words: "… or to take arms against a sea of troubles, and by opposing end them. To die, to sleep—no more—and by a sleep to say we end the heart-ache and the thousand natural shocks that flesh is heir to…"

Suddenly, I see Hamlet stabbing Polonius behind the arras and I hear Shakespeare's ghoulish laugh as he gets pleasure from the universal nature of his themes. "You too have been a murderer," he seems to whisper in my ear. I glance back up at the poor auditioner, droning on, until I can politely put an end to his speech. When I can stand it no longer I say, "Thank you, Richard. I'll post the callbacks outside the Theater office by the end of the week. Next."

By day's end I haven't found a decent Hamlet and my mind has grown weary of "To be or not to be." I have one more day to go in my search, and I say a small prayer that a miracle will occur and some English student, on leave from the Royal Shakespeare Company, will appear and pound out a brilliant one for me.

I take refuge in the library. The long, dark aisles comfort me— so much knowledge and wisdom speaks of a civilized world, albeit one, which seems relegated to dark, unused libraries. A small, round step-stool stands in the middle of the aisle and I sit down on it and grab whatever book happens to be in front of me. *Best North American Poets* is the title.

"Victoria?"

"Yes?"

I glance up to see Dennis standing in shadow at the end of the aisle. I don't rise up to greet him; instead I stay seated as he makes his way down the aisle to my side. Being squashed and doubled over on this tiny stool adds nothing to my already powerless position; but, I can't bring myself to stand up and look him in the eyes. When having my head level with his crotch becomes uncomfortable for him, he crouches next to me and gives me a strained and quizzical look.

"Hi," he says. This is the first time we have been together since the movie theater. He looks down at his feet. "What are you doing?"

"I'm casting a production of *Hamlet* for God's sake and I came here to escape the students. I've found the best place to escape students is the library."

He laughs.

"I can't find a Hamlet though. You know of anybody?" I ask.

"I'll think about it. ... O, that this too too sullied flesh would melt, Thaw, and resolve itself into a dew! Or that Everlasting had not fix'd his canon 'gainst self-slaughter!" he says beautifully.

"You'll do it!"

"No way! Did I say that?"

"I need you!"

"You'll find a student who can handle it. But I will help you if you need someone to sit in and give you a second opinion on things."

"Tom's helping me."

We are silent for a moment and uncomfortable.

"Oh," he says.

"But I'm sure I could use your help too."

Dennis clears his throat. "I wanted to tell you something. When I was in graduate school I wrote this silly little short story. Well, I guess it's not so silly, but I hadn't thought about it in years. I remembered it after I saw you in the movie theater. It was about this woman I loved one hundred years ago, then she came back again today and I recognized her. The characters time travel between a painful Victorian love affair and the present day. When I remembered that story I got chills. I almost couldn't believe it." His nervousness pleases me.

"A story? About a woman you loved one hundred years ago and she came back in this life?"

"I'm afraid so. It is hard to believe, I guess."

"Not for me it isn't."

"Well, I guess not for you. But for me it was a revelation." He looks down at the open book on my lap and I follow his glance to see a poem entitled *I Have Known You Twice*, glaring up at me. Jung must be smiling in his grave, for we have proven his Synchronicity Theory in that one moment. "Damn!"

"What is it?" Dennis asks.

Slowly I lift up the book and show him the page. I lower it and begin to read:

"I have known you twice
and unlike Heraclitus' River

you were the same both times.

While our eyes looked a different dog did bark;
The sun, in China, sent its beams a few degrees aslant.
The Moon was fifty minutes slow, while our hands met,
More solemn owls, mourned a stranger night;
The Universe was much enlarged they say;
and our lips touched
While different horns or sirens, cries or leaves
Floated in changing air.

Vain philosophers who do not love,
but observe streams or church steeples
Or look on mothers with a jaundiced eye:
I've scarce the wit to read them twice,
But when I do I find they lie.

So say we age, so say our eyes have changed,
The tissues of our hands worn off and been renewed;
So say our lips in tighter lines have grown
with knowledge's sure toll: I will agree.

Yet say we can in innocence love twice.
It has been done. Your love, like that grave law
That holds the earth in place, falls always here.

For I have known you twice,
and unlike Heraclitus' golden stream
you were the same both times."

I look up to see his eyes are closed as though lost in the words
I have just read. I tilt my body toward his seated form and kiss
him. I can do nothing else at that moment. I kiss him first on the
cheek and then on the mouth. It is a gentle kiss with closed lips,
soft and feathery. His eyes never open as his lips receive the kiss.
He doesn't pull away, I do.

He looks into my face. "I'm sorry," he says softly. "It is wrong. We just can't." He works his way up from the floor, I don't move. He smiles a half smile and then reaches into his briefcase and pulls out some sheets of old onion skin typing paper and holds them out to me. I take them from his hand and he walks away without looking back at me. He leaves me, sitting, once again, in confusion.

I perch on my stool, squashed and tiny, and glance down at the papers he placed in my hands. Typed with an old college typewriter, crinkled and torn on the corner, I read the line, "She stood in the drawing room, turned away from me, but from the reflection in the mirror above the mantelpiece, I knew I had caused her pain."

I feel anger rise up inside. He's playing with me, I think. Why did he give me this? To tear my heart into a million pieces? And how dare he kiss me and walk away—two times now! How dare he! Damn him to hell, the son-of-a-bitch!

"Fuck you," I whisper out loud to his retreating back. "Fuck you!"

Chapter Seventeen

During the last two decades of the twentieth century, Cornwall, Vermont expanded its borders onto a strip of highway the locals have dubbed "Miracle Mile." Unlike the older section of town near the university, where Gary's café is located, "Miracle Mile" is a monument to the American franchise. On one side of the street is Kmart, Taco Bell, ShopRite, Payless Shoes, CVS, a bowling alley, a Sunoco station, Appleby's, The Gap, Sears, two hair salons, a furniture store and a Wendy's. On the other side is Montgomery Wards, Home Depot, a brand new Barnes and Noble, Pizza Hut, Red Lobster, Grand Union, Pharmhouse, a Mobil station, Staples, Circuit City and a large office complex which houses among other things the insurance office that Sally works in. The traffic along this miracle is always horrendous.

Every week I visit the "Miracle Mile" to do my grocery shopping. Sometimes Sally meets me and we shop together. It takes the edge off of the dreary task. As usual she is standing in the vegetable section, leaning on her cart and staring at the door waiting impatiently for me to arrive. She is always ten minutes early and I am ten minutes late. She looks good, I think. Her face is less impatient than usual—fewer creases in her brow and around her mouth. Michael must be treating her well.

"Hey, Sally," I call to her and grab a cart.

"Hey, Victoria," she says and waves an ear of corn at me.

"Been waiting long?" I ask.

She stares at my face. "You look like shit," she says.

"Thanks a lot. You, on the other hand, look great."

"Thanks," she says. "How come you look so bad?"

"It's been a rough semester."

"I guess so."

I place a head of lettuce into my cart. "I'm losing it, Sally."

"Seriously?"

"I'm afraid so."

"Don't you have a therapist?" she asks.

"Yeah. So what?"

"Isn't he supposed to help you?"

"Yeah, but he's not."

Sally rubs an apple on her jeans and takes a bite. "So get a new one."

"Let's talk about something else. How's the insurance biz?"

"You're not going to like it," she says.

I walk over to the bakery section, grab a fresh honey glazed donut and put it in my mouth.

"I'm handling the insurance for the new Starbucks building."

"Traitor."

"Vicky, it's a big account. I can't turn it down. It won't make a whit of difference anyway. The store is going in."

"I know. It depresses me," I say. I look into my cart; it's empty except for the lettuce. Sally's cart is filling up rapidly. I take the last bite of donut and wipe my sticky fingers on my jeans.

"Don't you need anything?" she asks.

"I don't know." I push my cart to the side. "Maybe I'll just walk along with you while you shop. My heart's not in it." I reach into the bakery case for a custard-filled chocolate donut and take a huge bite.

"You better pay for those," says Sally.

"I will," I say and wipe a creamy blob of goo off my upper lip. I select another donut and hand it to her. "Here, they're good."

Sally takes it from my hand. "Michael likes plump women," she says.

"Keep him," I reply. "I think Gary is cheating on me."

Sally stops her cart and whips around to grab my upper arm. "No way, Victoria. It's not his style."

"I saw him with a beautiful blond," I say shaking myself free from her grasp.

"You're kidding! What were they doing?"

"Talking."

"That's it?"

"Yeah." I sit down heavily on a large cardboard box. Luckily it holds.

"Listen to me. Gary's not cheating on you. Are you cheating on him with what's his name? The married guy?"

"No." I look at the soup cans.

"Are you sure?"

"If President Clinton's clearly defined boundaries of adultery apply, the answer is no."

"You've had oral sex?"

Everyone in the soup aisle turns to look at us. I stare into the face of a six-year old boy, blush, and put my hands over my eyes and double over. "Shut up, Sally!" I force out in a loud, angry whisper between my fingers.

When I look up again, expecting to see Sally I find instead that I'm looking at Tom Banks and Sally has disappeared.

"Damn! I'll kill her!" I murmur. "Hi, Tom."

"Hey, Victoria. That was an interesting confession. If it's about Dennis I'll pretend I didn't hear. Could you hand me that can of chicken noodle?" He points to the selection in front of me.

Sheepishly, I pull it off the shelf and give it to him. He puts it in his cart and then graciously extends his hand to help me to standing. He touches his lower lip and stares at mine.

I look at him confused.

"You have something on your lip," he says and indicates the spot again.

I stick out my tongue and swish it around until I taste something sweet. "Thanks," I say. "You happen to see my friend Sally?"

"The red-head?"

"Yeah."

"She rounded the corner like a shot. I almost ran into her." He points his finger in the direction of her departure. "You staying around for the holidays?"

"I guess so," I reply. "I certainly don't want to go to Florida with Mom and Dad."

"So am I. Maybe we can get together."

"Yeah. Sounds good." I give him a wave and dash off in search of Sally. She is at the end of the next aisle and I sneak up behind her and give her hair a good yank.

"Ouch!"

"Serves you right."

"Victoria, I've only got one thing to say. Stop this affair with the married man right now."

"There isn't an affair. Besides he wrote a short story about us in college."

"What are you talking about? He didn't even know you in college," she says incredulously.

"That's what's so amazing! He wrote a short story about Victorian lovers. Just like us," I reply.

"Victoria, you have got to be kidding me. Have you lost all touch with reality?"

"No!"

"Let's look at the facts," Sally says. She holds up her hands and counts her fingers. "One, you are having hallucinations. Two, you are kissing a married man but it's not an affair. Three, Gary's talking to an unmarried woman and in your mind he is having an affair. Face it, Victoria you are a mess. You said so yourself. So just stop it now, Victoria!" Sally storms down the aisle—the wheels of her cart squeaking furiously.

"It's the truth, Sally. And I'm not a mess!"

"I don't believe you!" she yells but doesn't turn around.

Feeling rejected and definitely not hungry, I decide to leave. I'm afraid to be accused of shoplifting so I find a closed checkout counter and rush through it with my hands raised above my shoulders. When I get outside I realize that I ate two donuts and didn't pay for them, so technically I was shoplifting. Glancing back over my shoulder to see if I'm being followed, I race to my car, jump in and lock the door. I'm shaking and my heart is beating hard, but I refuse to go back inside and be further humiliated. "That's the last time I confide in Sally," I say. "The minute things are going well for her she becomes Miss High and Mighty." I look at myself in the rear view mirror—I still have a few donut crumbs around my mouth. I do look like shit. Thank God I've only got two more days to go until the students go home.

… A century had been lost, but I could still feel her heart beating close to mine. I could see her beautiful smile and hear the green taffeta of her dress crinkle as she moved across the floor. There would be no one in this place or time that could touch me as she had done one hundred years before.…

Ever since he gave it to me, Dennis's short story has been traveling with me, stuffed inside my large, black handbag. In the last two days alone this is the third time I've pulled it out and reread it.

Chapter Eighteen

The first snowfall comes on Christmas Eve. Sally is at her parents' home. Gary has gone to San Francisco to have Christmas with an old traveling friend. The town is empty and quiet and I have been enjoying the solitude up until now.

Christmas Eve alone. I won't do this again; it's ghastly. I try to bring up the memory of my encounter with Mr. Hawkins, the Central Park angel, to comfort me, but he seems awfully far away right now.

My finger dips into the eggnog, laced with brandy I bought specifically for the holiday season. I turn on the television. What else? Miracle on 34th Street. I can't bear it. I turn off the television. I pour another glass of brandy, minus the eggnog, and go out onto the porch and gaze at the Christmas lights that adorn every house in the neighborhood except mine. Every other house appears to me to ring with the joyous sounds of the season. Just my luck to move into a neighborhood without a Jewish family. Christmas carols come from the brightest house on the block, directly across the street from me. This year it seems that Santa and Jesus are on speaking terms both on the roof and the front lawn. Next year I am certain to bear witness to baby Santa in the manager and Jesus sliding down the chimney with Rudolf.

I decide that a walk would do me some good and I grab the bottle of brandy and a coat. It takes about a minute for me to head in the direction of Dennis's house. Drunk from the brandy I keep going, and tell myself that the liquor will warm my frozen fingers. I clutch the bottle and realize I've left the house without my cigarettes. I need a store run by Muslims if I want to find anything open. Maybe the Seven Eleven. I've got a few bucks in my pocket. I'm in luck, there's one a block away and it's on the way to Dennis's.

My masochistic streak has peaked. I know it. I'm totally conscious of the fact I am alone on Christmas Eve, drinking from a bottle of brandy, walking in the snow toward the house of a married man with a pregnant wife and searching for cigarettes from Muslims. There is something comforting about hitting bottom. You can relax. Alone and drunk the pressure's off. I look forward to finding a cigarette and breathing that thought deeply into my lungs. Yes! They are open. There are other people in the store as well. I will get my cigarette. I blink in the bright florescent lights. The little Iranian fellow is cheerful and gladly hands me a pack of Merits.

"Merry Christmas," I say.

"Oh. Merry Christmas to you," he says politely.

"I don't suppose you celebrate Christmas," I say.

"No," he says. "I don't suppose you do either, huh?"

"No," I lie.

Dennis's house is dark. Probably at his relatives. Being drunk I feel brave and sit on the front steps, put the bottle of brandy to my lips, and smoke another cigarette. Maybe I'll be arrested for stalking him. Maybe I should break in and lie down on their bed and pretend I'm making love with him. Even my alcohol-tipsy brain realizes the sickness of this thought and I scare myself enough to stand up and walk away from his house.

I light another cigarette and noiselessly wander down snow-padded streets, with only the sound of an occasional car to break the silence. The bottle of brandy is almost half-empty and I'm feeling warmer. The blue, red, green and yellow Christmas lights that adorn all the homes are beginning to blur around the edges. "Happy New Year," I call out to the silence. Then I giggle. "It's not New Year. It's Christmas! Happy Christmas!" I lift the bottle of brandy to the silent but well lit homes and take another swig. "Happy Christmas to you!"

Main Street is aglow with little white lights and decorated with wreaths and boughs of holly and red bows around the telephone poles. The snow is coming down harder now and the scene is definitely storybook. A banner, strung across the road reads: HAPPY HOLIDAYS.

The Café Bacchanal is dark. Being a Jewish-Buddhist Gary never decorated the outside of it. I press my nose to the glass and look inside. I miss Gary. Why didn't I go to San Francisco with him? He invited me. What's wrong with me? He's the best.

I sit in the doorway and light another cigarette. Sheltered from the falling snow I'm almost comfortable here. I take another swig of brandy and put the bottle down beside me. It's liberating being here like a bum.

"The only time I could do this is Christmas Eve. It's the only night of the year that Main Street is empty enough at 10:00 p.m. to get away with it." I'm talking out loud to myself. "Even the McDonalds is closed. Too bad, I could go for a cheeseburger."

I glance down at the bottle of brandy. About a third left. Shit! Did I drink that? Damn. I'm feeling sick.

"I've got to pee." I struggle to my feet and lean over to grab the bottle. I feel in my pockets to make sure the cigarettes are still there. I turn inward to face the door and shelter the match from the wind and light another cigarette. When I turn back to face the street I notice there are lots of lights dancing to and fro. I'm unsteady. Careful, Victoria. One foot in front of the other.

I walk to the next block and stare at the new STARBUCKS. "Fucking Starbucks. Fucking assholes. How dare you do that to Gary! He's the greatest. Fucking assholes. Gary deserves better than that!" I put the bottle of brandy down in the snow and lift up my coat. Then I unzip my jeans and pull them down. It's difficult to balance, but I manage to squat down in front of the sign that says: FUTURE HOME OF STARBUCKS. I look down at the pee to make sure it isn't landing on my feet. Oops, almost did. Better move the left one over. That's better.

I lift my face and look back into the street. What are those cops doing standing there? "Evening, gentlemen. Could you turn around while I pull up my pants?"

They turn around. I fall over onto my back and start laughing hysterically. "I landed in my pee!" I scream. Then I laugh even louder. The policemen turn around and walk over to me. The sight of them looking down at me, and knowing I'm lying on my back with my pants around my knees, dead drunk, sends me into hysterical laughter. I can't control it. I struggle to pull my pants over my hips. I roll over onto my stomach and push myself up to standing.

"You are drunk, lady," says the biggest cop.

"No shit, Sherlock," I say and clamp my hand over my mouth. "I'm not suppose to say shit to a cop!"

"And you peed on this private property," he adds.

"Yep," I say. "I drank a bottle of brandy and peed on Starbucks and now I'm going to get sick." I let out an enormous BLAACH and puke on his shoes. Suddenly dizzy, I double over and retch my guts out. I feel one cop on one arm, one cop on another arm and then I don't remember anything else.

… I am walking down a long hall. I am naked. Light emanates from underneath the doorways that line either side of the corridor. I walk slowly, marking my steps carefully. My feet produce no sound to break the silence. I am on a journey to nowhere. Suddenly I stop, but the floor keeps moving underneath of me drawing me onward against my control. Doors pass by me, moving on and on. I'm not afraid because I know I will stop when the time is right. I know I will reach out and open the door to find my lover waiting on the other side. The motion continues.

"Please stop," I beg. "Stop and let me choose my door." The words echo down empty hallways. "Stop and let me place my hand on the doorknob. Don't just keep moving on and on. My destiny is so close. It is almost in my hands."

A door flies open and I am thrust inside and flung onto the floor. In front of me stands a tall man. He is strong and handsome and powerful. I kneel before him and plead. I hold out my palms and see that fire dances inside of them, red flickers to light his face. As we watch the flames dance they grow cold and begin to die. "It is undernourished," I say to the tall man. "What am I to do with this light?" He holds out his palms toward me and we place our hands together in a perfect fit.

"See?" I say, "we have like palms, you and I." He pulls back his palms to reveal a burn on each one. Suddenly he slaps me with his burned hand, hard against my face, which sends me sprawling on the floor at his feet. "Do not talk to me about like palms," he says. "I have seen yours and they are full of pain."

"Please," I beg, but he grabs me and throws me down on the ground and laughs....

... I wake up shivering. I feel feverish. I open my eyes and look around. I'm lying on a hard mattress in a strange room. Holy Shit! Bars! I'm in jail. I pull my coat tighter around me. I got drunk, I remember that much. What did I do? Did I do something awful? Was I arrested for something terrible? I close my eyes.

The morning sun brings a cartoon headache: a hammer pounding over and over on the anvil in my head. I raise myself up onto my elbows and it pounds even harder. I'm cold and shivering. I'm in jail. I put my hands on my head hoping to contain the pain.

"Merry Christmas." A woman comes down the hall and stops in front of the cell. "You ready for a cup of coffee?"

"Yes," I whisper. She returns with a cup of black coffee. She opens the door and comes inside without closing it behind her. I guess she's not afraid of a prison break.

"You had a bad night," she says. "You can go home when you're ready."

"You mean I'm free to go?"

"Yep. Nobody's gonna hold a miserable, heartbroken woman on Christmas."

"Heartbroken?" I ask.

"Drunk and heartbroken. Cop said you kept saying Dennis then you'd say Gary. He figures you got enough trouble without getting arrested for peeing in public."

"Peeing?"

"You don't remember?"

"Maybe a little bit." I look down at the coffee. It isn't helping do much but warm my hands.

"Let me tell you what to do," she says. "Hair of the dog that bit you. You won't be right until you have some more alcohol. Trust me. Coffee won't take that headache away. But a Bloody Mary will."

"I just want to go home. Please don't tell anyone I was here."

"Not a word. You got money for a cab?"

"Not on me."

"I'll get one of the cops to drive you home. There aren't many on duty, but it's slow on Christmas."

She walks away and leaves me sitting on the bed. I'm too weak to stand, but boy do I have to pee. Can I make it home before I pee? It's going to be difficult. I stand up and shuffle out of the cell and down the hall in search of a bathroom. When I come back to the cell the woman is standing next to a cop. He doesn't say anything, he just points in the direction he wants me to go. When I begin my shuffle in that direction he comes in behind me and pushes me along. When he wants me to turn right he touches my right shoulder. Left gets a touch to the left shoulder.

Outside the sunlight is blinding. He opens the rear door of a cop car and when I climb in he shuts it behind me. Then he climbs in the front seat. "Four fourteen Maple Lane," I say. He drives me home without speaking a word. At home I climb out in silence and shuffle inside my house. I realize I left the front door unlocked all night. Everything appears to be untouched. Merry Christmas.

Chapter Nineteen

It's New Years Day, two days after Gary came back into town, and we are on our way to his parents' house for dinner. Herman and Lotte Dubitsky live in a colonial two-story in a tree-lined residential neighborhood near campus. They are retired from the University. He taught history, she mathematics.

"Hey, Mom," Gary says as she opens the front door for us.

"Hello, Mrs. Dubitsky," I say politely giving her a peck on the cheek as well.

"Hello, Victoria. Please call me Lotte. It's so nice to see you again." Her strong hands clasp mine. Her features—high, deeply chiseled cheekbones, heavy lidded eyes, and large, bony nose—overwhelm me with their power. I glance away and turn my attention to Gary as I extract my hands from hers.

"Where's Dad?" Gary asks.

"Probably in the kitchen," she replies.

I've been here once before for dinner. It is a comfortable house, one concerned more with reclining, propped up with a good book and a cup of coffee in your hands, than with matching wallpaper, rugs and couch covers. The sweet smell of pipe tobacco lingers in the air. The room is decorated with twenty or thirty pictures of their only child.

"Hey, Dad," Gary yells toward the kitchen.

"Come, have a seat, Victoria," says Lotte. "What can I get for you? A glass of wine?"

"Red wine would be nice," I say and sit as daintily as possible on the edge of a large well-cushioned sofa.

"Herman, get Victoria some red wine. How about you Gary?" Lotte calls in the direction of the kitchen.

"The same, thanks. Let me help you, Dad." Gary disappears, leaving me alone with Lotte, who sits down across from me and offers a platter of cheese and crackers. Gratefully, for something to do, I accept.

"How have you been, Victoria?"

A dry strand of cracker catches in my throat and I cough three times to clear it. "I've been doing well, thank you."

"Is my son good to you?" she asks with a smile.

"He's wonderful."

"I'm glad to see he's serious about someone so nice."

"Serious?" I ask.

"Is it?"

"Well..." I run my hands through my hair nervously.

"You two seem happy so I assumed...," she says.

"Well... we did talk about marriage. I proposed to him," I say.

For a moment the room becomes a vacuum and sucks out all the available oxygen—then Lotte catches her breath and says, "How modern. Gary never mentioned a thing."

Gary and his father come out of the kitchen with my wine. Gary hands me the glass and I smile stiffly.

"Herman," Lotte says, " Gary and Victoria are talking marriage." Gary turns his head quickly in my direction and glares.

"Victoria just told me," Lotte adds.

Although Herman doesn't look as taken aback as his wife, he immediately responds by saying, "You're not Jewish are you?"

His bluntness has caught me off guard. "No, no I'm not," I say. "I'm sorry. I shouldn't have said anything, we haven't actually decided one hundred percent." I'm blushing fiercely and feel like running from the room. I can't imagine what made me say that.

"I'm hardly Jewish myself, Dad," Gary says. "I don't go to synagogue. If I choose to marry Victoria the issue of Judaism is not going to enter into it."

His father turns on him slowly and without flinching he says, "You were born a Jew and you will die a Jew. There is no in between. The Nazis never asked me or my family if we attended synagogue before they hauled us off to the camps." He lifts the cuff of his shirt to display the number tattooed onto his wrist. Then he turns around and walks into the kitchen.

I can tell even Gary is shocked by the strength of his reaction. Gary sits down heavily beside me on the sofa and takes a big gulp out of his wineglass.

"Maybe I should go," I whisper.

"Give him time, Gary, he'll be okay. He's upset right now, but he'll adjust to it," says Lotte.

"Adjust to what?" Gary says and turns to me at last. "Victoria, what in God's name made you say that? We haven't seriously decided to get married."

Lotte graciously extends her hand to touch the back of mine and then says, "I'd better go and check on dinner," and disappears into the kitchen, leaving us alone.

"Your mom and I were just.... I'm so sorry."

We sit quietly and munch nervously on cheese and crackers as we wait for dinner to be served.

In a few minutes Lotte emerges with a roast chicken. Herman follows her with side dishes.

"Dinner," she says as she places the large bird onto the table. "Do you eat chicken, Victoria? I know Gary doesn't, so I made plenty of other things to eat as well."

We sit through the meal without mentioning the subject of marriage. Fortunately, I share not only Gary with Mr. and Mrs. Dubitsky, but also St. George University and it gives me a topic of conversation. Remembering how upset my mother was at Thanksgiving when I refused her turkey, I even take seconds of the chicken when offered.

As Lotte, Gary or myself make a point or offer an opinion, Herman comments on it, but never actually initiates the direction of the conversation. I consider blurting out, 'I'm really not a good Christian. I mean I wasn't even baptized, if that is any consolation,' but decide to keep that remark to myself.

After dinner we return to the living room for coffee and dessert and once again my horrible faux paux looms over us. Herman clears the dining table.

On the coffee table in front of me is a large photo album and I slide it onto my lap and open it up, hoping to find some neutral, happy topic of conversation.

The first page contains Gary's bare bottom and his happy fat-cheeked smiles as he lies in his bassinet and celebrates his first birthday.

Lotte was thirty-five when she had him—quite a bit older than the average first time mom of that generation. Herman looks radiant as he holds Gary up to the sky and mugs for the camera. He certainly wasn't unwanted, I think.

This is not a family that freely offers explanations of why only one child and why so late. Even Gary has never commented on that fact. Gary did tell me about his father and the camps, but said that Herman never talks about it. The horror cannot get past his lips. Gary's mother escaped from Germany as a child before the war started. She never suffered as her husband did.

"Gary sure was a cute little kid," I say.

"Wasn't he though?" Lotte says as she sits next to me on the sofa.

"Look at these high school pictures! What a riot! He looks like Greg Brady with that ridiculous flowered tie and the side burns."

"Oh please, Victoria," Gary says. "Greg Brady?"

"Who's that?" I ask, pointing to the picture of a stunning teenage girl on his arm at the prom.

"That's Jocelyn," Gary answers.

"She's beautiful." She also looks Jewish. At least more Jewish than I look, which isn't hard. I'll bet Herman liked her.

"You are beautiful, too," says Lotte.

"Thank you," I say gratefully.

I flip the pages and see pictures of Gary's long sojourn that took eight years and covered many different countries. India, Greece, Italy, France, Switzerland, Germany. I pause at a picture of him at the concentration camp at Dachau, in Bavaria.

"You visited there?" I ask.

"It's where Dad was," he answers. We are all silent as I look at the pictures.

Suddenly Herman bursts from the kitchen with the coffeepot and cups. He places them on the coffee table and sits down in a chair opposite me.

"You think I am a foolish old man," he says to me as he glances at the pictures on my lap.

"No, sir. I don't think that."

"Will you raise the children Jewish?" he asks.

I look to Gary for help.

"The children, if there are any, will be exposed to a number of different religions. They are free to choose whatever spiritual path suits them," Gary says.

"Religion is not like an overcoat," Herman says. "You do not put it on and then take it off when it doesn't fit quite right."

"Dad, I would not deny my children the right to know their Jewish heritage, or the right to worship as Jews. But, I'm not you, Dad."

"Meaning you did not suffer in the camp as I did?" Herman asks. "Is that what you are saying?"

"Mr. Dubitsky…" I say.

"What do you know of Judaism?" he shouts at me. "What do you know of how my people suffered? You smell the rotting, burning and tortured flesh of your people day and night and then we will talk!" He stands abruptly and walks out of the room and up the stairs.

"I'm so sorry, Victoria," Lotte says. "I've never seen him like this. Perhaps you two had better go for now." We all stand up and Lotte wraps her arms around Gary. With tears in her eyes she excuses herself from the room and goes upstairs to join her husband.

Gary doesn't say a word while we put on our coats. He doesn't say a word while we walk to the car. He doesn't say a word while we drive down the street. Finally I can't stand it anymore.

"Gary, I am sorry."

"Why did you do it? Did you think my parents would pressure me into marrying you? Why this desperation all of a sudden to get married?" he asks. His jaw clenches and he continues to stare straight ahead.

"I'm *sorry*," I repeat. "I don't know why I did it."

"Do you really want to get married, Victoria? Are you sure about us? Are you certain about me? Or are you running away?"

"Running away?" I ask. Then I snort. "Hardly."

"I need to know that you want to marry me because you love me and not because you are running away from Dennis."

"Dennis is nothing to me." I cough and stare out the window. "It's you I love."

I glance over at Gary. He looks back at me. We both look ahead. I reach over and put my hand on his thigh. He touches my hand for a moment and then puts his back on the steering wheel.

Chapter Twenty

It's bitter cold; people walk to classes with scarves over their faces, hats pulled down low, wearing bulky down coats and mittens. I pull the slip of paper out of my pocket and reread it. *Can we meet at Starbucks at 4:00 on Tuesday? Dennis.*

It is difficult to tell one person from another, even male from female, but I recognize Gary immediately even at distance. He is standing in front of Starbucks with only a hip length jacket on and staring at the façade. Someone is next to him, a woman I surmise by the colorful red, yellow and blue cap and the pink parka. Her slender legs, jeans and cowboy boots let me know it's Linda. She leans into the window, cups her hands around her face and peers into Starbucks. Then she turns back toward Gary, shrugs her shoulders, puts an arm around his waist and they walk toward the Café Bacchanal. I watch them until they disappear inside. I can hardly justify feeling jealous, after all I'm planning to enter enemy camp and have coffee with another man.

When they are gone I walk across the street and push open the door to Starbucks. The number of people inside surprises me. I see a student that used to hang at Gary's. He looks at me and then turns his face quickly in the opposite direction. He recognizes me even with the scarf across my mouth.

Slowly I make my way up to the counter. I pull the scarf down just enough to say, "A tall cappuccino, please," and glance guiltily behind me. So far no one else seems to recognize me.

The coffee is handed to me in a paper cup. Gary would never use paper unless the customer had said, "To Go." A large *No*

Smoking sign glares down at me. The clock says 4:10. I decide to take a seat on a stool in the corner at a counter that faces the front window. From here I should be able to see Dennis when he arrives. I slip the scarf from my face and put the steaming cup of coffee to my mouth, cradling it with both hands. It's hot, so I blow into it—when I lift my gaze back to the window I see Gary's face pressed against the glass.

He mouths, "Vicky?" I stare at him—like a mouse in a glue trap. I'm hoping if I stay perfectly still he'll go away and I'll be able to move again. The front door opens and Gary enters. Some of the students turn their heads, and others point at him and whisper behind their hands. Gary strides over to me, arriving in five steps.

"What the hell are you doing in here? You're a traitor," he says in a loud voice.

I glance around at the people staring at us. What can I say? I saw you with Linda? "Gary, I…"

"This is too weird for me, Vicky. I can't trust you anymore." He turns away from me and walks back outside.

I'm stunned. I decide to go after him. No, wait. What would I say? I slide off the stool and like a zombie I walk out the door. The cold air burns my lungs, shocking me back into reality. He can't trust me? I saw *them* together. How dare he say, he can't trust me! All I did was get a cup of coffee in Starbucks. When Gary disappears inside his café I return to Starbucks and climb back onto the stool and stare out the foggy window. I rub my hand around the glass in a circle to clear it a little; it doesn't help much. I put a palm to my forehead and rub hoping it will clear my mind, but it too is useless. I sense that people are purposely trying to pretend I'm not here and that they didn't witness what just transpired. How many of them heard the words, "I can't trust you anymore"? I'm too embarrassed to go back to the counter and get another cup of coffee, so I play with the paper cup until I've torn it into shreds. Then I pile all the shreds up into a little hill. I glance at the clock; it's 5:00. He's not coming.

***

The next day I leave my office and walk, numbly, toward the theater for rehearsal. January is dark, cold, endless, and mirrors my feelings exactly.

Suddenly, a large bank of snow, left by the plow, forms a road-block and sends me to the ground, knees first. My ungloved palms catch the jagged, dirty ice as books and papers form a ring around my body.

My fall feels like a personal slap-in-the-face, and tears form in my eyes as I twist around to sit on the mound of snow and rub my shin. For a moment I consider weeping out loud, freezing to death, and generally allowing myself the full expression of my miserable self. Only my pride and a deep sense of duty pick me up out of the dirt and snow and send me on my way to rehearsal. With my face red from the cold, my clothes rumpled and wet, my knees and hands bruised and my books clutched clumsily under my arm, I look up to see Dennis.

"Just the person I wanted to see. Sorry I didn't show up at Starbucks yesterday. My wife got sick and I had to pick up my daughter from her tiny tot ballet class. On your way to the theater?" he asks.

I nod and try to act nonchalant so he can't see my hurt and anger. "That's okay, I only waited a few minutes."

"I needed to commiserate, I'm having problems with my chairman. Can I join you? How's the production going?"

"You tell me."

We enter together; the cast is already assembled and awaiting my arrival. Dennis discreetly sits at the back of the theater as I make my way to the front.

"Sorry I'm late. Is everyone here?" I ask the disgruntled looking assemblage.

"We are all here," replies Jeff Munson, also known as Hamlet. He is smoking a cigarette and drinking a cup of coffee as he sits on the edge of the stage and drums his heels loudly against the wall. I realize how badly I want one of each.

"Jeff, can I bum a cigarette from you?"

"Sure. Feeling the pressure?"

"I guess. Okay let's go. We start with Act I Scene V. Does everybody know where he or she should be? Hamlet and Ghost on stage." I'm acutely aware of Dennis at each moment. I want to impress him. I don't want to look like a fool. "Do you guys remember the blocking?"

"I think so," Jeff says. Ghost stays silent.

As they climb up onto the stage I feel charged and powerful. I pace the floor. "The ghost of Hamlet's father is calling for revenge," I say in a loud voice. "He does not tell Hamlet how to revenge his death, but leaves this to Hamlet. How does Hamlet reconcile the deed? Claudius committed a sin when he killed Hamlet's father and married his mother, but isn't it true that Hamlet too will be sinning if he in turn kills Claudius? The question is—Can Hamlet become the instrument of providence and leave the solution of how to avenge his father's death in the hands of greater powers than himself? Ghost tells Hamlet, 'I am thy father's spirit. Doom'd for a certain term to walk the night, And for the day confin'd to fast in fires, Till the foul crimes done in my days of nature are burnt and purg'd away....' "

I pause and then I say, "Revenge, it seems, is not so simple."

I get the feeling the only one listening to my speech is Dennis. I am communicating something to Dennis, not to Jeff and Ghost. I grab another cigarette out of Jeff's pack without even asking him.

I walk up the aisle and sit down next to Dennis. I am acutely aware of the curve of his muscular thighs in the tight jeans he is wearing. All traces of past-life Victorian propriety are erased, becoming replaced by pure animal desire. Hamlet's father's ghost begins his speech (I'm vaguely aware that he isn't very good) and all I am thinking about is Dennis. When I reach my hand over and stroke his thigh, it actually feels beyond my control.

Dennis's leg twitches and he rubs his knee against mine, making a vain attempt to pretend that he isn't. I touch his knee and lightly caress the inside of it. My pelvis pushes into the back of the hard seat as I sense the slow, unmistakable grinding of his, beneath my fingertips. His hand brushes the top of mine and I turn my palm over cautiously, sending out sparks between the flesh. Our pelvises move in unison, ever so slightly and our eyes stare straight ahead at the stage. We are feigning innocence. I hear Ghost say,

> "Ay, that incestuous, that adulterate beast,
> With witchcraft of his wits, with traitorous gifts—
> O wicked wit and gifts, that have the power
> So to seduce!—won to his shameful lust
> The will of my most seeming-virtuous queen.
> O Hamlet, what a falling-off was there!..."

"Stop! Stop!" I cry. I have to stop Ghost from speaking these words that reveal my very soul. I jump up from my seat and race down the aisle to the front of the stage. For lack of anything logical to say to the actors I call out, "Isn't that blocking wrong? Jeff weren't you supposed to be downstage?"

"I don't think so." He sounds pissed off at being interrupted.

"Okay. Sorry. Go ahead." I turn to walk back to my seat and see that Dennis has left. In his place sits Tom.

"Hey, Victoria, sorry I'm late."

I nod at him then turn my face toward the stage.

"I saw Dennis on my way in," says Tom.

I nod again.

Tom turns his focus to the actors. "What's happening?"

"The ghost... that's what's happening."

I think, after all these years, I have a real understanding of what Hamlet is up against. In the play he is the only one who knows the truth, the only one who sees the ghost of his father—only Hamlet knows that the King, his uncle, is a murderer who has murdered his father and married his mother. All others around Hamlet act normally toward the King, flattering him and serving him, while Hamlet becomes more and more obsessed. In fact, Hamlet becomes so obsessed with the secret murder that he becomes embittered, antisocial, and raving mad, until others begin to fear that it is Hamlet himself who is a menace to the state. Only the audience shares with Hamlet a knowledge of the truth. Only the audience knows that it is the others who are deceived by their ignorance.

Sometimes I feel my only hope may be to die like Hamlet, and in my death affirm the tragic dignity which is man. This feeling only happens as I am watching the last act of the play, most of the time I feel pretty sorry for myself in a very unromantic way.

Chapter Twenty-One

I'm getting *married!"* Sally screeches over the phone, in my ear. "Unbelievable!"

"It is," I agree. It's seven o'clock Friday morning—not my idea of a wake-up call.

"You don't sound too excited," she says. "Aren't you happy for me?"

"Of course I am." I can't bear to talk about the wedding or babies or any of that stuff.

"You'll be my Maid of Honor, right?" Sally asks.

"Yeah."

"You'll help me pick out a dress, right?"

"Yeah."

"Great. I want you to go to the Bridal Shoppe with me tomorrow morning. I'll pick you up around eleven."

"Yeah. Okay. Eleven. Listen, Sally I've got to go. I've got to get ready for class."

"All right. See you tomorrow at eleven."

Cleopatra jumps onto my lap and purrs loudly. "Marriage," I say aloud to no one but the cat. "What a ridiculous notion. To think I wanted to marry Gary." Cleopatra looks at me. "The truth is, Cleopatra, I miss him."

Sally is ecstatic when she picks me up Saturday to go to the local Bridal Shoppe to look at dresses.

"Sally, when's the date?"

"May 1st."

"That's three months away. "Why the rush to get married? You haven't known each other very long."

"When it's right, you just know."

Her remark hurts. I look down at my hands and feel my cheeks get hot. Instead of a snapping turtle that strikes out when poked at, I feel like the kind that digs deeper into its shell. She doesn't notice.

"I want something white, flowing and very romantic. I thought the bridesmaids should be in pink."

I hate pink.

"You look so good in pink, don't you think?"

I don't reply.

She glances over at me. "Come on, it'll be fun."

We enter the Bridal Shoppe, my face grim, Sally's glowing, and walk past rows of white and pastel dresses.

"May I help you?" the saleslady asks. She speaks automatically to Sally who just radiates bride.

"Yes, please."

The saleslady turns toward me and sizes me up like a raptor circling a rabbit. I judge her to be about sixty. She's had plenty of years to sense a woman that endangers her commission. She turns her back on me and smiles at Sally.

Sally is oblivious, and prances around like a kid at Christmas. "How about this one?" she asks me.

"That's stunning," says the saleslady. The two of them huddle around a froo-froo wad of white stuff. "Isn't that just perfect. What a lovely bride she'll be," she says as she looks at me with a sugary smile.

"Not really my style." Simultaneously their eyes tell me they don't like me at all. The saleslady selects another dress and shows it to Sally. "Now don't you think this is just perfect for her?" she asks me. Her strategy is to win me over so that I'll help her make the sale. I frown.

"Lovely," coos Sally. "Isn't it lovely, Victoria?"

"Well…" I say trying to play the game the best I can.

"How's this?" The saleslady pulls a dowdy, plain white dress off the rack. It reminds me of a prom dress from 1965 with the bust line protruding and the empire waist.

"Yuck," I say. The saleslady drops her 10% commission smile and glares.

"Don't mind her," says Sally. "She's got man trouble right now. Why don't we just browse for awhile and when I see something I like I'll come and get you."

"Fine." The saleslady gives me another cold look and walks away.

"How about a Maid of Honor dress? Do you see anything you like, Vicky?"

"I don't want to spoil this for you. Why don't I just sit over there and you go ahead and look? If you see something you like let me know and I'll try it on."

"Okay, Victoria. I'm not going to let you bring me down."

"Give me a minute, Sally. I'll cheer up."

Sally walks back to the saleslady and touches her on the shoulder. Like a couple of conspirators they walk over to some wedding dresses and talk quietly.

I turn to the clothes rack and paw through the dresses. I feel like pouting and crying; I'm like a tired five-year-old who wants to be playing and instead finds her Saturday being used up by shopping with her mother. "How about this dress?" I yell to Sally on the other side of the store. I pull a dress from the rack. It is the only funky one in the store—it is short, sexy and stylish.

"That's for a prom or something! Have you lost your mind?" Sally yells back at me.

"Sorry. I thought it was kinda cute," I say.

"Yeah. Maybe for MTV or something. You are impossible. Sit down and I will bring dresses to you and you tell me if you like them. Okay?"

I sit on a satin lounge chair, as instructed, and Sally parades dress after dress by me. Pink ones with bows, blue ones with ribbons, yellow ones with lace—they blur in front of my eyes and I drift in and out of reality. My other lives run through my brain like a tape loop. At one point, as I imagine I am the mean old Roman slave owner, sitting on a satin lounge chair and picking out a Maid of Honor dress, I laugh out loud. I become hysterical with this image and I put my face in my hands to quiet the laughter.

"What the hell is wrong with you?" Sally asks.

"Nothing." I return my attention to the symbols of purity and innocence that pass before my eyes. Only one meets with my approval and Sally hangs the others back on the rack and studies the one I've deigned to consider.

"I like this," she says. "It is quite elegant. The other girls should look good in it as well."

"Good. How much is it?" I ask.

She stares at the price tag. "Five hundred dollars." I practically fall off my chair.

"Five hundred dollars for a dress I'll never wear again?" The store falls silent and everyone turns to look at me. Sally shrinks in utter embarrassment.

The saleslady walks over to us and looks as though she wants me dead. "Perhaps you should leave until you are more certain of what you want," she says through clenched teeth.

"Fine," I reply smugly. I march out of the store with my humiliated friend at my heels.

"Thrown out of a fucking bridal shop!" Sally yells when we get outside. "Victoria, get a grip! You got us kicked out of a fucking bridal shop. What the hell is wrong with you?"

"What the hell is wrong with people who spend thousands and thousands of dollars on symbols that are supposed to declare how much they love each other to the rest of the world and then fifty percent of them get divorced anyway?"

Sally sticks her tongue out at me and we walk in silence to the car. When we get there I pause before opening the door. "I'm sorry, Sally. Whatever dress you want me in is fine. I'll wear it, I promise. Why don't you just take me home now? I'm not fit company."

"No shit." Sally climbs in behind the wheel and we drive home in silence.

Gary's house is dark when I drive up to it. It's four o'clock on Saturday afternoon; I wanted to slip a note under his door, thinking he'd be at the café. The note says *I Love You*. That's all, just *I Love You. Victoria*. I'm surprised to see his car in the driveway. I get out of my car and hesitate at the doorstep. It's a cloudy winter afternoon and if he's home I would expect to see a light on. Maybe he's not feeling well. Maybe I should call first. I've left messages and he hasn't returned them. I put my hand on the doorknob. Slowly I open the door a crack and listen for a sound. I smell coffee. I hear nothing.

I push the door open wider. Two weeks ago I would have walked in without thinking and yelled, "Gary!" Two weeks ago I would have known where he was. I feel like an intruder. I step into the foyer. The smell of coffee is stronger. I walk toward the kitchen thinking he might be in there. A fresh pot of coffee sits on the counter, but no sign of Gary.

I consider slipping the note under the coffee maker, but decide to keep going. I need to see him again. To explain everything and hear him say, "I forgive you."

I walk upstairs slowly, listening for a sound. When I reach the top stair I think I hear something coming from his bedroom. The door is slightly ajar so I walk lightly to it and push it open. "Gary?"

Gary and Linda are lying in bed, naked. He is on top of her, his face pressed against her stomach. They turn to look at me but don't try to hide their naked flesh.

"Goddamnit, Victoria," Gary says.

I'm getting flashbacks of Amiele. I'm a child—girlish and naïve. I've burst in on a forbidden world, one usually reserved for sophisticated adults, one where I don't belong.

"How could you just walk in like this?" he asks, lifting himself off Linda, keeping the sheet wrapped around his torso—toga-like.

"You called me a traitor.... I'm not the traitor here." Linda frees herself from him and sits up. I notice her breasts. They are firm and round and even seated her stomach doesn't pouf at all.

Gary starts toward me.

"Get away from me," I yell. The note falls from my hand onto the floor. I run down the stairs, out the front door and into the car before I realize I dropped it. "Shit!" How could I be such a fool?

Chapter Twenty-Two

At 4:00 on opening day, a huge snowstorm begins to blanket the town. I'm already at the theater, checking with the costume designer on last minute details, making sure the tech crew is ready and all the lighting changes are complete. The cast arrives at 6:00 and the show opens at 8:00.

I have mixed feelings about this snowstorm—opening nights tend to be pretty disastrous, it could be a blessing to have a small crowd. On the other hand, the excitement of opening night is never repeated as the production continues, and it is nice to milk the theatrical hubbub for all it's worth that first night. Unlike Hamlet, I decide to put it in the hands of providence. Blizzard or not the show must go on.

It is almost dark when I step outside at 4:30 for a breath of air. The snow swirls in the street lamps; it seems that at least two or three inches have accumulated in the last hour. It is lonely behind the theater and it mirrors my feelings. Between the trucks parked in the loading ramp and the overhang, I find some relief from the weather, and brushing the slight accumulation of snow from the cement wall, I sit and light a cigarette. I find that I am longing to act. Not just to direct, but to be the one on stage who actually says the words and brings the audience to tears and laughter. "I could be a great Queen," I whisper....

"Oh Hamlet, speak no more!
Thou turn'st mine eyes into my very soul,
And there I see such black and grained spots
As will not leave their tinct..."

I wonder if I will get flowers from Gary? Maybe he has decided to apologize. I go inside to see if some flowers have been sent to the theater for me.

Nothing has come. I retreat to my office to freshen up a bit. Many parents will be on hand tonight and I have to look presentable. It is an effort; I am most definitely in a jeans and sweatshirt mood. Behind my door hangs a tailored pantsuit back from the cleaners. I peel off my jeans as a knock sounds.

"Yes. Just a minute." Whoever it is doesn't answer, so I quickly zip up my pants and throw my sweatshirt back on. When I open the door I see Dennis standing on the other side. He doesn't have flowers, he doesn't have a bottle of wine—he merely stands quietly and raises his eyebrows when I look at him.

"Hi," I say.

"Hi," he replies. "Good luck tonight."

"You coming?"

"Tomorrow. I can't tonight." He doesn't make a move to enter.

"Come on in." I gesture and stand aside.

"For a minute. You probably have to get going." He walks in but doesn't move away from the door. I get the distinct feeling he is frightened to be alone with me in this room.

"I have to be back at the theater by 6:00 to do a warm-up for the actors."

"Is it going well? Do you feel good about the production?"

"Yes. I guess so. Better than I thought I would. Thank God I had directed *Hamlet* in graduate school. I was in no state of mind to handle a first time production of it."

"I guess not," he says.

I want to kill him. I can't believe how quickly he can evoke that feeling in me. How can he stand in front of me time after time without acknowledging the emotions between us? It makes me crazy to witness the pseudo-control. Breathe Vicky. "You want to sit down for a minute?"

"Sure," he says and plops himself on the couch. I sit next to him knee to knee, turned so we can see one another.

He doesn't speak, but I see the pressure build up inside of him. He fascinates me. I develop a cold scientific eye, and study him as a seismologist might look at a developing crack in the earth. He is stuck, I realize, and his inactivity is his only defense to the turmoil of his emotions brewing beneath the surface. I can almost hear his thoughts:

If I do this, then this will happen. If I do that, then that will happen. If I do this and that then God knows what will happen. Should I do what I should do? Or what I'm supposed to do? I guess I'd better not do anything, that way I won't get into trouble.

"Why are you here?" I ask.

"To…" He pauses. "To express my best wishes for the show."

"Thanks. Anything else?" I reach my hand over and touch his fingertips. His hands seem large and powerful to me and I want them on me. I want them in my hair, on my breasts. I want him to consume me. I want him to love me. My thoughts frighten me, but instead of pulling me back, they cause me to act—if I act quickly I can't hear myself think. I throw my arms around him and kiss him—the force thrusts him backward. I am on top of him, and the energy flies between us as he grabs onto me.

I feel his mouth on mine, moist and hot. His breath is furious and demanding. His mouth presses harder, his wet lips devour mine and our teeth meet sending a bolt of electricity into my aching thighs. His lips slide down onto my throat. I turn my face away, presenting myself like a lioness to her mate. For a moment our breath stills in silent anticipation of the power he now wields over me.

His tongue follows the path of my neck, slowly savoring each taste of flesh. When he reaches my hard nipples he unleashes a power that can no longer be contained and we claw and grab as though by sheer will we could enter one another and forget the realities of our world. His strong hands go around my throat, and then down my back. Mine grab his head and clutch his smooth hair.

I whisper in his ear, through clenched teeth. "I want you inside of me. Please, oh my God, please." With those words my spirit leaves my body and I lose consciousness.

When I return to Earth I am naked. He thrusts into me, hard and demanding. My desire to contain him in every cell of my body is so great that even my returning thrusts don't feel like enough, and I grasp onto him with raw force longing to drag him into my soul for eternity.

soul for eternity. A moan slides from his lips and with it, the walls he has erected to keep his heart from touching mine collapse. A rush of breath and sound forces itself from his body deep into the recesses of mine and I feel the brush of his lips against my ear, "I love you," lands so softly that I wonder if he knew he said it.

Dennis becomes pliable and limp against me and his skin follows the curves of my abdomen as it rises and falls underneath his. His eyes tell me that I am in the moment where men are weakened and lovers reveal their true nature. I close my eyes to awaken my other senses fully to the experience. When they open again I see that his eyes have closed to me.

A warm bath of falling in and away rushes over us and I feel his lips touch gently upon my nose. He opens his eyes once again and I stare into them until they become tunnels. I travel further and further back through them and the deeper I go the more I sense fear rise up into my chest. The weight of his body presses my bony spine against the cold, wooden floor and forces the breath from my lungs. Danger, my heart cries out.

I push at his broad chest to free myself from the pressure of his heavy weight; immediately our naked flesh becomes a part of us once again. Dennis sits up quickly. His body becomes rigid as he reaches for his clothes. For some minutes neither one of us speaks.

Finally he says, "I can't believe I did that. I'm so sorry. I swore to myself to stay away." It is the one thing that enrages me more than anything else he could say; a dismissal. A refusal of the feelings once again. I'm too angry to cry and I shake instead. Dennis stands up, and he walks to the door of my office and exits without a word. It is 5:50 and I'm sitting on the floor in the middle of my office, trembling and wondering how I'm going to get to the theater and survive the night.

Chapter Twenty-Three

The familiarity of Ted's office brings me a measure of comfort when I see him the next day. Last night I stood at the back of the theater through the entire production of *Hamlet*, but I remember little of it. I shook hands with some parents, praised the students and went home. There are no words to put to the feelings that Dennis evoked in me last night.

Ted stares patiently at me, but I find it hard to tell him about the lovemaking. I close my eyes and I can smell Dennis, hear Dennis, feel Dennis, taste Dennis. Every pore of his body is imprinted upon me. I long for him so deeply. He repulses me in equal measure. I want to run away, change my name and never be in this town again. I realize that I am afraid. Deeply afraid of him and all he makes me feel.

"Vicky? What happened?"

"I am afraid of him," I reply. "Very afraid."

"Why?" Ted asks.

"We had sex. Sex of a nature that no words can explain. Passionate, lustful, dangerous, fulfilling and hungry sex. I felt things I've never felt before. Heaven and hell. I'm sorry. That's the best I can do to explain it to you. That's it." I lie down on his couch and turn away from him. I want to crawl back into the womb and start all over again.

Ted remains silent, waiting to see what I'll say next.

A few minutes later his patience is rewarded.

"Ted?"

"Yes?"

"An image keeps coming up. It's so strange because it doesn't seem to have anything to do with anything."

"What is it?"

"I'm standing in front of a gate," I say. "I'm not sure where it is, but it is summer, because the sun is shining and the flowers are blooming. The flowers are cheerful, but I feel a bit anxious."

"Vicky, you've gone over a month without any images. Please, deal with this and stop retreating into fantasy."

"I have on long pants and a short jacket with gold trim and men's boots. I think I have on some kind of hat as well. I think I'm a sea captain. There is a house behind the gate. It is the house I am going to. I don't think I live there. A woman lives there. I know this woman, but I have been gone a long time and I am a little nervous about seeing her again, but I'm not sure why."

I wonder where this is taking me. What an odd picture to be forming in my mind. I know what this woman inside the house will look like. She is blonde and full-figured. She wears her hair up on her head, but it falls casually about her face as it comes undone. She has a broad mouth and wide blue eyes. Her fair skin has pink blotches on it. The sea captain thinks she is beautiful. Well, I guess if the sea captain is me, then I think she is beautiful.

… My heavy boots step slowly up the stone path toward the house. Rose scented air—petal ripened—rises up from either side of the path. My heart races ahead of me in anticipation of the future, followed by my body, stiffened by fear of the unknown. I do not knock, but gingerly turn the iron latch handle and push open the wooden door.

Inside the room, beside the hearth, is a woman busying herself with iron pots. A crude wooden dining table stands between us, and my entry has been quiet enough that she does not notice my arrival. Step by step, I put my boots one in front of the other with silent purpose. Still my presence goes unnoticed.

As I draw near her, my hand reaches for her back, and although I have not yet actually touched her, she wheels around, disturbed by her senses.

"AAAHHHH!" she screams and drops the kettle from her hands onto her foot. She hops to the chair as screaming, cursing words fly from her throat. "How dare you sneak up on me like that!" Her eyes reflect the pain and anger she feels.

I kneel at her feet in deference and take the injured toe in my hand to comfort it. Her rage will not be so easily calmed, and she grabs the foot away and kicks me with the healthy one.

"You leave without a goodbye and return without a hello! Am I to forgive you so easily for this? Is my heart so soft that your boots can tromp in and out of it on a whim?"

I hang my head in shame, but my fingers slyly reach out for her foot and this time she lets me draw it to my mouth. My lips feather it at first, and then go stronger, as if to suck the pain from her wound. My tongue darts between the spaces as my eyes gaze upward to her face. Anger has been replaced by pleasure, and I know my magic has worked on her once again. She cannot resist me. And I cannot resist her.

My hands slide up her strong legs. Legs that stand and squat, legs that are necessary to complete all the tasks required by living in this time and place. Machinery has not replaced the duties performed by these legs—they are rooted to the earth, connected to its rhythms.

The uppermost thighs are moistened and made humid by her sexuality, my lips reach her mouth at the exact moment my hands reach her damp hairs. My chest heaves with passion, hers surrenders. I lift her in my arms and carry her out of the room into the bedroom. The way to the bed is familiar to me. I have been here many times before....

"Victoria, did you have sex with Dennis to get back at Gary? I know you are angry with Gary, but you aren't dealing with the feelings at all," I hear Ted say through the fog in my mind.

I lay her on the bed and slide her skirt up around her waist. I lower my body on top of her as we claw and tear at the obstructive clothing. Her mouth opens to receive my eager tongue, but I do not have time to accommodate it, for instead of a kiss, a scream bursts forth as she pushes against my heavy chest to free herself.

I turn just in time to see her knife-wielding husband descend upon us. My naked body springs from the bed, but I see no means of escape as his massive frame blocks my exit. He thrusts me against the wall, but I am agile and quicker than he is, and as my knee rises to deliver a fierce jab to his groin, my hand knocks the knife free, and I run from the bedroom.

Two steps from the front door I am grabbed from behind and thrown to the floor, nearly knocking me unconscious. He presses down and his strong hands grip my throat. He drives my skull into the ground.

She screams and runs into the room clutching the knife he dropped. She positions herself to deliver a murderous blow to his massive back. In a final show of strength I thrust him upward at the same moment she thrusts downward, and instead of her husband's back, the knife lands in my throat and pins me to the floor.

"Do you think Gary has been fair with you? Victoria, I can't help you if you don't talk to me."

My breath comes heavy. My body turns and twists.

In the silence that follows I feel the life drain from my body. My chest heaves as it grasps its last breath. She has murdered me. I have been murdered by the one I love most.

As my soul rises I can see the events before me quite clearly. Her moment of realization of what she has done is followed by a wail of pain that shatters even my silenced heart into a million pieces. She runs outside and flings herself on the ground in agony. Her grief resonates throughout my spirit and I hover above her, attempting to offer solace. She cannot feel me and I float away from Earth longing only to see her again....

"Vicky, are you all right? I suggest you see a psychiatrist. You need a medical diagnosis. More than likely you also need antidepressants."

My eyes open and I look over at Ted. "What? What did you say?"

"You need to see a psychiatrist. I can't prescribe the medication I think you need, so I'm giving you a referral to a psychiatrist. Her name is Doctor Farrell. Dr. Maura Farrell. She's very good." Ted reaches for a pad of paper and writes her name and phone number. "I'll call her and let her know I've referred you."

"Antidepressants? Are you serious?"

"Very."

"I won't take them."

"I think you should. It's not a failure to admit you need medication."

"I think I need to leave." Slowly I stand up and move away from the couch.

"Take it." Ted hands me the piece of paper.

I take the piece of paper from his hand. "I won't call her."

"Think about it, Victoria. Just consider it."

I shake my head and walk out of the office.

Chapter Twenty-Four

At four-thirty the next day, I leave my office, bundled in a long, down coat, and step outside into the fading winter light. The stiff brown trees are illuminated momentarily by a weak sun shining low in the pale blue sky. I notice the silhouette of a large, barren oak against the Catholic Church on the edge of campus. I know it's the Catholic Church that Dennis attends because one Sunday, when I was on my way to the theater to rehearse *Hamlet*, I saw him entering with his family.

Maybe Dennis's energy will be contained somewhere inside and I will be able to feel it again without actually seeing him.

The world is strangely silent as I draw closer to the massive stone building, and in a trance, continue up its steps. The bells ring three times as I pull on the iron door handle and enter the dark, cold atrium. To my left is a stairway, to my right a hallway leads to the offices. I stand quietly listening for sounds. A chair leg being scraped against the cold floor echoes from somewhere inside.

An elderly woman, bent in a painful looking posture, dips her crooked fingers into a marble basin and crosses herself before entering the church. I watch her carefully and mimic her act, hesitating a moment because my fingers (along with the rest of me) have never been baptized. Dipping them in the freezing water sends a thrill down my spine, and I cross myself and bow as I have seen others do in the movies and on television. I pull my down hood up over my head in deference to the large, bloody Jesus nailed painfully at the altar and slowly make my way up the aisle to get closer to his contorted body.

His peaceful face, hanging high above me, draws me to him, and I bravely climb the stairs to bring myself nearer and stare into his downcast eyes. Dying poinsettias rim the edge, and the smell of stale incense assaults my nostrils. No questions or answers enter my brain, and this blankness feels foreign to me. There has been no peace inside my soul for many months now. Instead of thoughts, I reach my arms out to the side of my body, and imagine what it must have felt like to be him, nailed and bleeding, praised and scorned, forgotten by God and ever remembered by mortals. "Why have you forsaken me?" he asked. Or did he, I wonder? Perhaps it was only lesser men who questioned this fate, who imagined that this state of ultimate humiliation was one of abandonment.

I back away from him and walk down the steps into the aisle glancing about to notice a handful of others scattered throughout the large church, heads bowed in prayer. I take a seat in the fourth row, clutch my icy palms together and place them on the back of the pew in front of me. Slowly my head comes down upon them and I pray for the understanding that will bring me relief from this pain of remembering. This pain of longing for Dennis. Footsteps echo quietly down the passageway toward the altar.

For a moment I am afraid that I shouldn't be here, that it is against the Catholic Church's rules to allow me to sit in the pews. The footsteps stop before reaching me and I peek underneath my arm to see who is there; perhaps it is an authority figure come to take me away and scold me. I can't quite make out the person so I raise my head above my arm, to get a better look.

Dennis stands absolutely still, eyes glued upon Jesus, hands clasped together at his stomach. A small cry escapes my lips and a wave of nausea rises from my bowels into my chest as I thrust my head deep into my arms. *Please, let him think I am a grieving widow*, I pray.

For a couple of minutes there is no sound from his direction so I peek, once again, underneath my folded arm to see where he is. He is seated now, head bowed, face in hands.

My spirit flies to him, as the spirit of the sea captain circled the body of his weeping lover. I'm sorry, I hear myself say again and again. I want to run to him, hold him in my arms and make it better. Heal the wounds we have created. The pain in my chest crushes my will as I realize that my comfort would only bring him more agony and uncertainty. My arms around him will only increase his sorrow. I can not heal that which I have wounded—it seems I can only wound more and more. My love for him feels like a poison, sweet to the lips and deadly to the insides.

But he must feel as I do. Why else would he be here in the middle of the week praying? Rustling clothing alerts me to his movement and I lift my face when I hear his footsteps once again. He does not exit as he came in, but walks to the other end of the pew and down the outside. A throat clears.

I rise, stiffened by the hard wooden bench and the cold air, and carefully move sideways across the aisle into the pews across from me. I still can't see him, so I inch my way down until I can hear his voice more clearly. I can't make out the words, but the hum of his inflection rings in my ears. Where are the voices coming from? I'm all the way at the other side of the church. I sit down and swing my body around to see down the side aisle. Dennis's back is to me, but I see now that he is talking to a priest. A few more people have entered the church. Some of the office workers have stopped in to say goodnight to Jesus before they leave and light a candle for a dead relative or lost soul.

What the hell is Dennis doing here? My God, I think, who is he anyway? I don't know this man at all. How many brothers and sisters does he have? Are his parents still alive? Does he come here often? Dennis and the Priest walk away from me and disappear out of sight.

Boldly I stand up and walk in their direction, hoping my hood and large bulky coat will obscure my identity should they decide to turn around and start back this way. An alcove filled with lighted candles beckons to my right. Behind it stands a confessional. I pause at the candles and cross myself as I glance to my left to try and observe their whereabouts.

The hum of voices reaches my ears once again. They are here somewhere. I can tell it is Dennis. I inch closer to the confessional but the words are still unclear. Is he in there? I glance around to see if anyone can see me as I move in closer and closer until I am standing right next to the booth. No one can see me here in the darkness in this alcove, so I lean in even further. Now, I can hear his words more clearly.

"Forgive me Father, for I have sinned. It has been ten years since my last confession," he says quietly.

"Ten years?" the Father repeats. "You have never taken confession on Sunday?"

"Ten years," Dennis says again.

"And why was it so important to you after all these years that I hear your confession today?" asks the Priest.

I know I should run away. I know even if I am not a Catholic I am committing the biggest sin I can imagine committing in this life: the invasion of another person's privacy. I lean in closer, but I hear nothing. Dennis is silent. Afraid that he knows I'm here, I move closer to the candles, ready to light one and throw myself on the floor prostrate in sorrow, should he change his mind and suddenly exit the booth. I move in closer again when I hear the Priest's voice. Now I'm only a foot away.

"Yes? What is it?" the Priest asks again.

"I... I... I had sex with someone other than my wife. But that isn't the problem. Of course, that's a problem, but the problem is that I don't understand why. I mean why do I think about her? Why does she have this power over me to confuse me and make me do these things? Do you believe in reincarnation, Father?" Dennis is blurting all this out in strangled, breathless words. I can't believe he said the part about reincarnation.

"Reincarnation?" asks the Priest. "I consider myself a modern man. A priest who can relate to and understand the needs of the many college students who are in this parish." He hesitates. "And yet, I can't see what reincarnation has to do with the act of adultery. It sounds like you need to look clearly at your marriage."

"Father, I asked for you to hear my confession because I've always felt comfortable with you in the past, and I know you do wonderful work in the community. But..." he pauses, "this is probably not the place to come and discuss reincarnation." The Priest is silent. "Suddenly I feel foolish and realize I shouldn't have come here. I was raised in the Church and it seemed the only place I could safely talk about this."

"If you and your wife wish to have counseling for your marital problems I would be happy to assist you. As to reincarnation, I'm afraid I can't help you much. I'm not a believer," the Priest says.

"I remember how comforting it was as a child to be able to tell the Priest anything and have him rid me of my sins with a few Hail Mary's," Dennis says.

He's in big trouble now, I think. He's pushing it. I can't bear to leave even though that part about talking safely has really made me feel guilty.

"I can't rid you of your sins," Father says. "You have to do that. I think you had better consider marriage counseling. Today, I want you to say fifteen Hail Mary's and pray for half an hour on where you have gone astray. Then I want you to schedule an appointment for marital counseling."

"I'm sorry, Father. I will consider what you said about the counseling. Thank you."

Suddenly the door to the booth opens up and Dennis emerges. I run to a pew and kneel, face down. Dennis walks slowly toward me and for a brief moment my heart races, thinking he somehow knows I'm here.

He sits down two pews in front of me and bows his head. I hold my breath for fear of being discovered. For five minutes I kneel motionless until the pain in my knees becomes unbearable. Slowly I raise myself to a seated position. Dennis has not moved. Quietly I stand up and inch my way to the end of the aisle, ready to make my escape. As I near the aisle a strangled sob reaches my ears. Can he be crying? God, how I long to hold him. I reach my hand out to touch his back, but I can't. He might as well be miles away. I might as well be in spirit form and he in body. We can give each other no comfort.

I turn away and hurry from the cold, dark church into the cold, dark world.

Chapter Twenty-Five

For the last three nights I have had the same dream:

It is very hot on the crowded plane. Bodies jam the small seats, my white-gloved hands clutch together as I look out over the propellers. Something is wrong, I can tell. The plane should have left the ground long ago. Things have been wrong quite often lately, and I am leaving Germany, finally convinced that Hitler means to annihilate all the Jews. It has been inconceivable to so many of us that such a thing could really happen; we hope we are mistaken, and Hitler's promise of a strong Germany includes all of us. But the acts of aggression become impossible to ignore, even for the unwilling to see, and one by one we disappear.

On the plane the passengers are restless. None of them, as far as I can tell, are Jewish. Seated next to me is a man—there are only a few men on the plane. He seems a bit edgy, but then we all are. I wipe the perspiration from my brow with a handkerchief and smile at him. He returns the smile, but his gaze is miles away.

"Achtung. Achtung." A Nazi soldier strides onto the plane and orders us to be quiet. "Heil Hitler," he cries out. He scans the seats with his eyes, piercing our flesh as though he could tell our very souls by glancing at them. My heart races, my stomach feels sick. "There is a traitor on this plane and we will find him. Or her," he adds looking at me. "If he, or she, does not give up within ten seconds I will begin to kill everyone on the plane."

I am stunned. The mothers begin to scream and the children begin to cry. To prove his point he grabs the man seated next to me and puts a bullet through his head. BANG. No thought, no remorse. Then he hands him to the Nazis standing behind him who toss him off the plane. "Again, I will kill all of you if the traitor does not give himself up."

"No," I scream. "It is me you want. I'm the traitor. I'm the traitor here." What has propelled me to do this? I want the violence to stop. I want the killing to stop. Perhaps if they kill me they will spare the children. I do not say anything else, I just stand there shaking, beyond all thought and feeling. I am staring the Devil in the face and I know it. I sense he is winning, for I can do nothing but shake and tremble and place myself into his hands. He grabs me from my seat and slaps my face.

"You are a traitor? I think not. But perhaps you are just a Jewish whore trying to save the life of her lover," he says. "Does anyone want her?" he asks the Nazis standing behind him. He pushes me onto the next Nazi who pushes me onto the next Nazi who grabs my arms and thrusts me out the plane and into his waiting car. He climbs into the back seat next to me and signals the driver to take us away....

Upon awakening my head feels foggy and doesn't clear all day, so I don't notice the white piece of paper taped to my office door until I'm almost upon it. The sight of the paper frightens me and I duck into my office before reading it.

I don't understand this. I sense that perhaps you do? Can we talk? Dennis.

I tear up the note and throw it into my wastebasket. I recognize this feeling and I try to push it away. It is a longing to reach out to Dennis. A longing to explain this to him—to touch him, to look into his eyes and make everything okay.

"Goddamnit!" I close my eyes to relive our moment in the Catholic Church, but it doesn't have the power to rescue me from his desire to see me again. With hardened fists pressed into the desk, I resolve not to answer the note.

Not only am I avoiding Dennis but also it has been two weeks since I've seen Ted. I canceled last week's appointment because I couldn't bear him telling me to take anti-depressants. Gary hasn't called and I've resigned myself that it is over between us.

Thanks to Sally, bridal magazines are stacking up around my house. Every time she comes over she brings a new one. The last time went something like this:

"Come on, Victoria," she whined, "you've got to get into the spirit of this and help me. Look at how beautiful they are." She pointed to a model in BRIDES all decked out like Scarlet O'Hara standing on the steps of Tara beneath an old magnolia tree. "Tell me that deep inside some tiny part of you that doesn't love that."

I grabbed the magazine out of her hands and gave the photograph a good long stare. "You know something, Sally, when I look at her all I see are black slaves being sold on the auction block so Big Daddy could buy her that dress."

I'm amazed we are still friends. I've decided to ask Tom to be my date for the wedding. I'm out of options. If he turns me down I'll kill myself. I swear it.

"Tom?" I knock on his office door.

"Yeah. Come in."

"Tom. I'll be blunt." I sit down on the chair and stare at him. "I need a date on May 1st. My friend Sally—you remember the red-head at the grocery store? She's getting married. I'm the Maid of Honor, and I recently caught my boyfriend in bed with another woman. Will you go with me?"

Tom leans back and smiles. God, if he got anymore relaxed and easygoing he'd be an alien. "Sure, why not?"

I exhale and clasp my hands together. "Oh, thank you."

"I'm not even insulted that I'm your mercy date," he says.

"Oh, God, Tom. I didn't mean that. I'm sorry."

"It's okay, Victoria."

"Tom, I'm just an asshole lately. Don't mind me."

"I don't." He smiles again and leans over the desk to touch my hand. "I'm going to miss this place. I've grown to prefer the pace over the hectic life in Boston."

"You're kidding?" I ask.

"Not at all. I've enjoyed my time here."

"Except for...."

"Except for the horrible incident with *The Maids*, of course."

"I'll be sorry to see you go."

"I'm sorry I have to go. I've got a great class of acting students this semester. Jeff did a mean Hamlet."

"He did." There's a knock on the door.

"Come in," says Tom. Dennis pokes his head in. Around his neck, in a carrier, is a baby. Tom looks at me and sees the look of horror on my face.

"Hey, Tom." Dennis pauses when he sees me. "Victoria."

"Hi, Dennis," I say trying to sound nonchalant.

"Gregory," says Tom. "I haven't seen him since he was born. Boy, he's gotten big."

Dennis sits in the chair next to me and Gregory whimpers on his chest. He brushes Gregory's smooth, rosy cheek with his hand, opens the zipper on Gregory's snowsuit and removes his little cap.

"Can I hold him?" I ask.

"Sure," he replies and lifts him out of the carrier and puts him in my arms.

The sweet, soft scent of baby powder rises into my nostrils. I lower my nose to the top of his head to breathe it in fully, and brush my lips across his brow. His little fingers reach up and clutch onto my nose and slip in between my lips. "Aren't you beautiful," I coo.

A longing rises in me, so deep, that even I don't know where it's coming from. I draw Gregory tightly to my chest and kiss his forehead. Dennis looks at me and for an agonizing minute we reflect silently on the child I hold between us. Then, without a word, he draws the baby from my arms.

I stand up and turn my attention to Tom. "Thanks for coming with me to Sally's wedding. I'd better go."

"Glad to help out," says Tom.

Chapter Twenty-Six

For me, spring begins April 1st when the sun comes out, the temperature suddenly reaches 60 degrees and I see a robin and three crocuses. It might snow tomorrow, but today is beautiful and I vow that this will be the year I begin my very own flower garden. Annuals, perennials, rose bushes—all will bloom spectacularly and the neighbors will be envious.

"What I lack in Christmas decorations, I'll make up for in flowers," I say aloud as I walk the yard making plans to illuminate my surroundings in yellow, red, pink and purple flashes of color. I have replaced Sally's bridal magazines with gardening magazines and pour out my fantasies of the ideal life into them.

There is so much that I've never gotten around to: Italian tiles in the kitchen, a skylight in the bathroom, and a cozy woodstove in the living room. Where has the time gone? In the three years I've owned this house I have accomplished nothing. I continue to pace the lawn planning the exact location of the gladioli and irises. Maybe some tomato plants. I sit in the grass and close my eyes. Slowly my resolve to make the best garden in my neighborhood drifts away.

I feel myself leaving the Earth plane. I am going to my Nowhere Place, the place I have been drawn to over and over in my dreamy life. In this place, all boundaries are removed and I touch Dennis without restraint and without anger. In this place, there are no wives or husbands, no knives, or children—there is no past and there is no future. In this place is peace and silence, although many ideas are communicated there.

I haven't traveled to this place in a long time, yet I can close my eyes and summon it to me. In this place Dennis and I kneel and are anointed in love by something with no form and no shape. His love is returned to me freely until it fills my senses so completely that it spills from me into the vast realms. A river runs from our love and is lined with flowers and grass, brilliant and intense. The sky is full of birds made real by our love; the clouds shaped to speak the words of our love. We bathe naked in the river of love, our bodies beautiful and strong. Our passion takes shape and we slide and slip over one another like fish at play. It is not him that enters me in this lovemaking—nor is it me that enters him—we enter one another as equals: a lusty, blessed union of delight.

I can spend many hours in this place, but it is always the Earth's gravity that brings me back again. When I open my eyes the flowers I have planned to adorn my own garden pale by comparison. The clouds I stare up at make scary faces, and I turn away. My own body is angular and hard with none of the softness of my dream-body. I roll onto my side and see the spiders and ants scurry on blades of grass. Their homes are as insignificant as my own.

Chapter Twenty-Seven

Final exams loom before the students as the semester draws to a close. The days are warmer now, the campus is covered in bodies, studying and taking in the sun. A golden retriever runs across my path, following a Frisbee.

George walks up behind me and taps me on the shoulder. "Faculty meeting in fifteen minutes." God, I hate faculty meetings. He must have radar. He knows exactly how to track me down.

"I'll be there," I say and smile. When he has departed I frown. "Yuck."

The usual cast of characters is assembled. Over the school year, Lester Barnes grew a mustache and now reminds me of Snidely Whiplash. Karen Low gained twenty-five more pounds, is wearing a navy blue beret and looks like the Staypuff Marshmallow Girl. Nick Tarkington took off the tip of his index finger when he was building the set for *Hamlet*. Pam Witherspoon got pregnant but not married and Tom Banks looks exactly the same. I look pretty rough. I'm wearing jeans, sneakers, and a pullover sweater. I know I'm pushing the acceptable clothing limit, but I can't seem to get much enthusiasm up for personal grooming these days.

"We'll all be sorry to see Tom go. He's been a real asset to the department," says George. "Your student evaluations were excellent. You'll be sorely missed."

"Thanks, George. I'll miss being here. I've enjoyed my time," says Tom.

George shifts in his seat and studies the papers in front of him. He clears his throat and pushes the papers away from his body, then gathers them back up and straightens the corners. George is rarely at a loss for words and he seems anxious. I look over at Tom. He gives me a puzzled expression. George clears his throat again.

"The first thing on our agenda is the student choices for next year's productions," says George. "*Merchant of Venice*, which I assume Victoria will direct, is acceptable."

I nod at George to indicate I'm okay with the idea of directing Shakespeare's play. But I wonder what he means by acceptable. "Acceptable?" I say.

"*Loose Ends* and *Caligula* are not. *Loose Ends* is about abortion. Too dangerous. And *Caligula*... is obviously about Caligula, and that's all I need say about that. Given what happened last fall with *The Maids* I've decided to veto the last two choices."

"You can't be serious," says Tom. "Isn't it the students' right to choose what they see produced?"

"Yes, in the past it has been. Not any longer."

"George," says Lester. "This isn't only your decision. You're going to cause more unrest this way. The students will flip out."

"We need a year of theater that will unify this community. The most controversial playwrights I want next year are Tennessee Williams and Oscar Wilde."

"Both of whom are homosexual," I say.

"I don't care. Nobody is going to object to *The Glass Menagerie* or *The Importance of Being Ernest*," says George.

"What? Just like that?" I say.

"George," says Karen. "I don't agree."

"Would the painting department censor its students' work for being controversial?" asks Tom.

"I don't care. The painting majors aren't being killed for their product," says George.

"If you do this, George, you are letting the small-minded bastards win. They can't be allowed to win this fight. Art must express the full range of the human condition and experience. Life is often ugly, confusing and always challenging. It's the duty of the artist to reflect that struggle, not to shy away from it," says Tom.

George stares at Tom, his lips clenched tight. The staring lasts about thirty seconds—it appears to be a standoff until George says, "Tom, what you say may carry a certain weight. But unfortunately, you are no longer part of this regime."

"Regime? What is this, the Third Fucking Reich? And who are you, Adolf Fucking Hitler?" I blurt out.

Everyone turns and stares at me in amazement. I'm trembling so hard my ass muscles are vibrating. Suddenly Pam gasps and squeals.

"Pam," I say with exasperation, "It's about time someone said—"

"Oh no!" she cries. "My water broke!"

Pam's announcement puts an end to our discussion.

The following afternoon I'm standing on my doorstep wearing a pink satin gown with a huge pink bow tied at the back, poofy sleeves, and pink dyed-to-match pumps. My hair is pulled back on the sides and secured with flowered barrettes. The air is chilly today; a stiff wind tosses large cumulus clouds through the sky. The wind also threatens my hair and makes goosebumps stand up on my bare arms. Two sorority sisters walk up the path next door and stare at me. I shift my body away from them. I wish Tom would get here.

A car comes around the corner and pulls up. Tom steps out and walks toward the door. I half expect him to present me with a wrist corsage and be sprouting a recent outbreak of acne. He picks the tie up off his chest and says, "My only one."

I lift the skirt off my thigh and say, "And this is my only one. Thank God. Let's get out of here."

"You look…" he says.

I scrunch up my nose.

"Wholesome."

"Great."

The Methodist church is filling up when we arrive. Sally's mother, a tall overweight woman with a take-charge manner, hustles over to me. "You must be Victoria. You're late," she says. "The girls are in the bride's room downstairs in the basement. Sally's been waiting for you."

She grabs my hand, leads me through the foyer of the church and points to the stairs. "Down there and to your left." I turn, smile lamely at Tom and wave. I feel bad leaving him alone, he doesn't know a soul.

Sally is standing in the middle of the room. Her dress takes up half of the available space and the other half is filled with pink satin-clad girls and women ranging in age from five to forty-five. The air is saturated with the odor of perfume and hairspray.

"Victoria. I know you always keep me waiting, but grooms are supposed to leave brides at the altar," Sally says, trying to cover her annoyance.

"Sorry." The other bridesmaids stop talking for a moment to look at me. When they've given me the once-over they resume their conversations.

"Can everybody leave for a moment so Victoria and I can be alone?" Sally asks. The others stare at me but don't move. "Please?" Slowly they file out. When the door has shut behind the last pink satin bow, Sally turns to me. "How do I look?"

"You look great, Sally. Really glowing."

"That's good, because I'm pregnant." She looks intensely at my face, judging my reaction.

"You're serious? How come you never said anything? How many months?"

"Almost four. Do I show?"

I stand back and look at her. Her full figure hides the belly. "No, not at all. I'm sure nobody will know."

"Nobody does know. Not even Michael."

I fall down into an easy chair. "Michael doesn't know. Are you kidding?"

"I was afraid to tell him."

"Afraid to tell him? My God, Sally, in an hour you'll be married to him for the rest of your life for better or for worse until death do you part. Why the hell didn't you tell him?"

"Because I was afraid he'd tell me to abort it or something. Or he wouldn't want to marry me." Tears fall down her cheeks and she wipes them on the back of her hand.

"He's going to find out soon enough. Didn't you have a hard time explaining the morning sickness?"

"I felt fine; he never suspected a thing. I figured after we're married he'll be happy about it," Sally says. "That was really stupid, wasn't it? And now it's too late to change things."

She stands in the center of the room, afraid to sit and mess up the beautiful dress and train. She reminds me of the doll cake I used to beg my mother to buy me when I was a little girl. The doll's huge crinoline-cage skirt was made of cake and iced with buttercream. The doll was so beautiful; I had to have one. "Yep, it's too late now."

"What if he regrets marrying me?" The tears flow faster down her cheeks. I stand up and put my thumb over a tear and wipe it away for her. Then I give her a big hug.

"Sally, he loves you. He'll love your baby. Now stop thinking about it and enjoy the day."

"Really?" she asks with a hopeful look.

"Really."

"You're the best Maid of Honor and friend I could ever have."

"And you are the best Scarlet O'Hara bride, so go out there and keep saying to yourself, 'Frankly, Scarlet, I don't give a damn.'"

"Isn't that his line?" she asks with a whimper.

I shake my head. "Today, his only important line is, 'I do.' "

Tom and I are sitting outside the Villa Capri, hiding behind the hedges and smoking a joint given to him by Michael's best man. We are also drinking from a bottle of champagne he stole from the kitchen. I'm leaning against the outbuilding that houses the garbage cans, my shoes are off, my stockings have a run in them and the flowered barrettes have long since been lost in the grass. I suspect my pink satin is permanently ruined with grass stains. Tom's tie is tucked into the pocket of his jacket and the top button of his shirt is open. He takes a toke off the joint, coughs and hands it to me. I take an even larger toke, but don't cough.

"When was the last time you smoked pot?" I ask.

"About a year ago."

"Last time I smoked was when Michael brought some over to my house. You think Michael's a pothead?" I ask.

"Maybe," says Tom. "It's good quality."

"Soon he's going to have a pot head Junior."

"What?"

"Sally's pregnant. Four months. Michael doesn't know."

"You're kidding? She married him and didn't tell him?" He laughs that goofy marijuana laugh that continues on too long then sputters out.

"What's so funny?"

"Life."

"What else?"

"The fact that idiotic George is worried about offending people, when reality is far more offensive than anything ever written in a play."

"Half the stuff that occurs in life—if you showed it as it really is, not faked or dramatized or anything—people couldn't watch it. They couldn't bear to see it happen. They need to be removed from it to observe it. That's what drama does, it removes the audience from reality just far enough so they can bear to look at the truth behind the situation," I say.

"A brilliant analysis." Tom takes the joint from my fingers.

"I know, I'm always brilliant when I'm stoned. That's the beauty of it." I take a big swig from the bottle of champagne and pass it over to Tom, who also takes a swig. "Tom, do you have a girl-friend?"

"No."

"Oh. Do you have a cigarette?"

"No."

"What do you have?"

"An offer." He stubs the end of the joint out on the lawn. "Serious."

I laugh.

"No, really."

"I can be serious." I smile. I look at his lips. I wonder if I should kiss him.

"I want you to move to Boston."

"You want me to move to Boston and you want to take my job here, is that it?"

"No. I'm ready to leave. I want you to be the Artistic Director of a repertory theater company I'm involved with. I don't want to do it and I think you'd be great."

"I'm a fucking tenured professor. I can't just up and leave."

"Why not?"

"Because."

"Because? Because you respect our fearless department chairman so much and you want to do 'safe plays' for the rest of your life? You could do anything you wanted to in Boston. You could discover new talent. You could direct Shakespeare anyway you want. Come on, it would be great."

"I just can't. I live here."

"What's holding you?"

"You're stoned and drunk and tomorrow you'll regret asking me," I say.

"I won't. What's holding you? Don't waste your talent."

I look at him. His face is flushed. I never noticed how blue his eyes are before this. Almost piercing blue. They are kind eyes, gentle eyes. Familiar eyes. I never noticed before how familiar they seem. Suddenly I feel very sad. I can hardly look at him. "Tom, you think I have talent?"

"I know it. Remember the off Broadway production of *Little Angels* you starred in? What was it? Twelve years ago?"

"You're kidding. You saw that?"

"You were... brilliant."

"I was humiliated."

"Humiliated?"

"John Perry, the theater critic, was in the audience, in the front row. He left during the first act, right after my huge, long monologue." I look away from him, embarrassed by the memory.

"And... so...?"

"He hated me."

"Did he write a scathing review?"

"No, he just left. He never wrote a word. I think he died shortly afterwards. Fitting since he killed my dreams of being an actress. I decided to go for my Ph.D. after that. I'll suffer my humiliations offstage, thank you."

"Victoria. Your monologue was astonishing. I still remember your entrance—it pierced my heart."

"Really? I entered with a scream."

"It not only pierced my heart, it pierced John Perry's heart. He suffered a heart attack that night. When he left he was probably on his way to the hospital with chest pains."

"Chest pains? I thought he hated me," I say.

"Just like a fucking actor. The whole world revolves around you."

"Holy shit! John Perry had a heart attack. I didn't suck after all!"

"So you can stop blaming John Perry for this Ph.D. thing. It's time to realize you don't suck." He reaches across, I start to hand him the joint, but he takes my hand. "Come to Boston and start feeling alive again."

Chapter Twenty-Eight

I drag myself to Ted's office. "So Victoria, what do you want to talk about today?" he asks.

I think for a moment, then I say, "I've been dreaming about Nazis."

"Nazis?" He obviously did not expect that because an expression registers across his face I've never seen before.

"Well nobody likes Nazis," I say. "Anybody in their right mind would be afraid of a Nazi. Don't tell me you don't fear Nazis?"

"Not really, not on a gut level. With me it is more intellectual than a pure fear response," he says.

"That is such bullshit. If a Nazi came in here and said that he was going to take you to a concentration camp, you wouldn't be afraid?"

"It's not my dream."

"But I wasn't afraid; in my dream I stood up to them."

"Stood up to who?" he asks.

"The Nazis, of course."

"I've got a really unique idea, Victoria. Why don't we talk about Gary? Or Dennis? Or your job? Or Sally getting married? Or anything that might have even the remotest connection to your life!"

"I sense some anger, Ted."

"That's a start. At least it keeps us in the present."

I stand up and walk to the window and look out onto Main Street. Three blocks away is Gary's café. Two blocks away is where I peed in front of Starbucks and the police hauled me off to jail. I never even told Ted about that. "What if...." I start then pause.

"What if?"

"What if they are connected, the past and the present? What if I can't understand the present until I clear up the past?"

"Your childhood, yes. Nazis, no. Unless your parents are Nazis, I don't want to talk about it right now. Answer one question for me, Victoria. If you could be anywhere, doing anything, with anyone right now, what would you choose?"

"I don't know. I'm feeling very afraid right now. Where I used to have my feet on solid ground, now I don't know what to believe. Ever since I met Dennis my world has gone into complete chaos."

"In my line of work I see people in obsessive love relationships quite often. He or she enters your life, and you are so overwhelmed by your feelings for them that nothing else matters. Marriages fall apart, betrayals happen—the strength of the attraction between the lovers is far too powerful for them to resist. It always signals something deeper. Some underlying cause that isn't being addressed."

"A cop-out, is that what you are saying?"

"If you want to put it that way."

"What if there is more to it, Ted? What if it is karma? Gary believes in karma. 'As you sow so shall you reap'—even Jesus believed in karma." I hear myself say, "It's Universal Law."

"It isn't relevant."

"I said fuck Universal Law, too, but what if karma is the force that draws those obsessed people together? What if sometimes they can find forgiveness and the karma is overcome, but other times they can't forgive the person or heal the wounds they've created and they just end up creating more karma?"

"Okay, Victoria. You win. Tell me about Nazis."

"I will then." I lie back on the sofa and close my eyes. "Ted, what I remember is being forced off a plane by some Nazis and thrown into the back seat of a black automobile."

"Do the Nazis remind you of your family or anyone you know?" Ted asks.

"Nope. They are Nazis. Fucking scary Nazis—in living color."

… We drive through the bleak German countryside, and although I stare out of the window of the big, black automobile, I notice nothing. The Nazi next to me hasn't spoken a word since he signaled the driver to take us home, and his silence increases the tension until it is almost more than I can bear. I want to turn and look at him, to see his face clearly, but I am afraid to move, certain that it will mean physical harm to do so. Why hasn't he said anything?

I feel his hand on my thigh. The shaking in my body becomes so profound that I cannot conceal it. "I won't hurt you," he says. "Look at me." Slowly I turn my face to him, but my gaze is downward. "Look at me," he repeats and my trembling face lifts upward. "You are either brave or foolish. Which is it?"

"Neither," I say.

"Neither? I don't think so. You are a Jew, aren't you?"

I don't reply. I can't reply. The trembling increases. Then he does something that shocks me so totally I cannot find a place to process it in my brain. He puts his arm around me and leans my head into his chest. I weep into his chest and he allows it. The only comfort I can find is in the arms of my most bitter enemy.

We drive past gates and barbed wire. The smell is unbearable. How can people live here? My glance through the window of the car has frightened me so profoundly that I huddle down, refusing to see. I do not want to know where I am. The car pulls up in front of a wood building and the Nazi hustles me inside, covering me with his coat.

This is where I will be tortured, I think. He leads me to a chair, removes the coat, and when I look around I see that I am sitting in his kitchen. I do not speak. I am paralyzed by fear.

"You will live here," he says. "I need a cook and a housekeeper. You will be those for me." I do not look at him. He walks over to me and puts his hand under my chin. He kisses me roughly on the mouth. "Perhaps you will also do other things for me," he says. "It's either here, or out there." He points through the kitchen window that looks out over the camp. "It's your choice."

I don't answer. I am afraid he will strike me, but he doesn't. Instead he leads me to his bedroom.

"Rest now," he says. He walks out of the bedroom and leaves me alone.

I cannot be awake, and I cannot be asleep. I slip in and out of my body, until my bladder calls me to full consciousness. Quietly I rise from the bed hoping to find a toilet. It is a dirty little room off the bedroom and I urinate quickly and crawl back into the bed. There is nowhere for me to go. There is nothing for me to do. My fate is in the hands of this Nazi. I can only wait until he returns. Eventually I fall asleep and wake only as he lies down on the bed next to me. His breath smells of alcohol and tobacco. I pretend I am sleeping but his hand strokes my breast.

"Did you sleep well?" he asks. Again I don't answer him. What can I possibly say? His hand strokes my breast harder and begins to open the buttons on my dress. I feel his hot breath on my face and chest. His mouth gropes for my nipple and he takes it playfully. Against my will I am becoming aroused and I clench my teeth, determined to feel nothing. His hand slides into my panties and I feel his erection against my leg. He rolls his body on top of me and works his penis between my thighs. His hands spread me and I feel his penetration.

"You don't like it?" he asks. "I think you do," he answers himself. The fucking goes on for a long time, until he finally ejaculates and rolls himself off of me. I turn away from him and huddle in a ball, tears running down my cheeks, the salty taste in my mouth. "You're crying?" he asks. He curls his body next to me and puts his arms around me. He strokes my hair just before he passes out into a deep sleep....

As these images fill my mind my body tenses and twitches. They are coming rapidly, and I become consumed by them. When I can bear it no more I open my eyes. Ted stands over me, but I see Nazis. Ted grabs my arm, but I feel Nazis holding me. "No!" I scream. As he leans over to comfort me I kick him full-strength in the belly and send him to the floor.

Chapter Twenty-Nine

W hen the air returned to Ted's lungs I agreed to spend three days in Towering Pines under the supervision of Dr. Maura Farrell. I figured it was the least I could do for sending him to his knees.

Towering Pines was built in the 1960's when facilities of this type flourished. It consists of an ugly concrete eight-story main building with four or five outbuildings scattered about on the once well manicured lawn. At one time it housed hundreds of mentally ill patients. Many of the buildings are now closed and have gone into a state of disrepair, but the main building is still in operation. I agreed to go so long as I could have a private room, and since in Ted's mind he had sent me here for rest and recuperation he didn't object. I told him I'd pay the extra out of pocket if he couldn't convince my insurance company it was medically necessary. So that evening I am sitting up in my single bed and staring at the—what else?—towering pines outside my window. The sunlight is almost gone and the trees appear as large, dark, ghostly shadows swaying gently in the wind.

In the hallway I hear an occasional shriek, cough, laugh and sneeze. In its heyday the facility housed depressed housewives, overdosed teenagers, husbands who had been fired after twenty-five years on the job. Today, I suspect it is home to only the most depraved souls, and me. The door to my bedroom doesn't lock and I imagine all the crazies standing outside thinking up ways to kill me. The valium they gave me wins over my nervousness and I lie back onto the clean sheets and relax. God, I hope nobody from work finds out. I called in sick—not sick in the head.

Within minutes I fall into an uneasy sleep, and when I awaken in a state of terror it is pitch black outside. Suddenly, a sharp pain stabs me in the abdomen. The pain increases. Grabbing a blanket to wrap around my body, I rise from the bed and walk over to the window. As my eyes adjust to the light I hear a voice say, *The healing is in the remembering.*

I know what he is talking about. My mind has been filled with the thoughts and images of Nazis. "What if the wound opens and never closes again?" I say to the voice. "The scab has been picked at so many times that I am afraid this time it won't heal over and I will be left a limp doll, my soul having bled out of my heart with nothing strong enough to repair it."

You are strong. You are strong. The voice reminds me, over and over. *Listen to me,* it whispers in the night. *Listen to me,* it screams to me in the night. *I have a story to tell. There is only the healing. There is only the healing.*

Shivers rise in my body and I bring the blanket underneath my chin. I wonder if it is Hamlet's ghost that haunts me. But I know better, this is my ghost; I own this ghost, not Hamlet. I close my eyes, but my fear of the blackness beneath my eyelids forces them open.

"What do you want? Go away."

Silence. A stab in my womb. *Listen to me.* The wind rustles the leaves outside the window. *Listen to me. I am fear. I am fear.*

A child's eyes loom before me large and vacant. They call to me, *What's happening to me?*

I fall down on my knees in prayer. "God, please tell me what this fear? What is this fear?" I hear a voice, a voice rising from deep within me. Soon, I am standing before a large white light, so brilliant I am consumed by the Charge. I know it is the Light of God. I hear the words:

Remember how you have laid on your back in the sun? You lift your hand to block the sun's rays and find that your tiny hand can cover the sun and create darkness on your face. The sun is so large, and yet you think your hand has blocked it from your face.

Fear is like your hand—fear blocks the light of God and makes you think it isn't reaching you. But the fear is so infintessimal compared to the power of God that it could never block it. It merely makes you think you have—just as your hand thinks it has covered the entire sun. Stand back a little and you will see your hand in its true proportion.

I lift my hand to block out the powerful light of God but the light shines through it. "I am ready," I say to the Light. "No matter how great my fear, I know I am not alone."

I spread the blanket on the floor and lay my body on it. I give myself up to Universal Law. There are no secrets in the universe. Who is it we are hiding ourselves away from? Who do we think we are fooling?

"I am ready. I am ready." Fear grips my throat. I push it down remembering the Light is always with me. A feeling rises inside of me, familiar only to a place so deeply buried that my conscious mind cannot retrieve it, but my unconscious mind knows it intimately. I am in a place where the systematic, cold-blooded, calculated annihilation, degradation and torture of six million people will be carried out with precise detail. Where molecules of burning flesh daily fill your nose, and the sounds of tortured bodies fill your ears. Where Hell is a reality and Heaven a madman's dream.

… I never go outside of his home. Never. Days pass in an endless sweep of confusion and terror. My Nazi has grown fond of me in a strange way. I sense that I am his only connection to the something human still left in him, and he clings to it ferociously. He has become so sickened by what he witnesses day in and day out that he is being driven mad as slowly and painfully as if he were one of the Jewish victims housed in the camp. He alternates between tenderness and control, when he feels too much tenderness he bashes it down with the power he knows he has over me.

Our sexuality has become both sinful and lustful. He needs me to need him and sex is the only way he can truly control me.

I loathe him, and the guilt I feel as my sexual excitement rises wrecks havoc in my soul. I think of killing him, although it would not free me. There will never be freedom for me, I realize. There will be only endless sex and cleaning in this house of stale air and sin.

My bare feet have spent almost nine months moving between the bedroom and the kitchen of this prison home. The double bed, covered by yellowing sheets and musty blankets, has become my refuge and I lay on my back hour after hour and stare at the gray ceiling with its cracked and falling plaster. Sometimes I turn onto my side and blow away the dust that has accumulated on the nightstand, the dust I am here to clean away for my captor. My captor who is also my savior. It is only because of him that I am not one of the shaved-head Jews of the camp.

The only window that overlooks the camp is above the kitchen sink. When I do the dishes I do not look out upon my people. Instead I stare into the sink, memorizing the stains and counting the holes in the drain—twenty-two in a circular fashion. I stare into the dirty dishwater and train my mind to go blank.

One day as my mind drifts, I forget to focus downward into the sink and allow my gaze to rise and my eyes to look upon the camp and its people. Standing before me, naked in the dust and dirt, are children huddled and crying. One boy looks up toward my window, his eyes so large that they consume me with their pain and I stare into them as though they were the windows that led straight to Hell. I become transfixed by the horror and I cannot move. My Nazi sneaks up behind me and puts his arms around my waist and kisses me on the cheek. He is in a tender mood and he turns me around.

"I want to have a child with you," he says. "We could have a baby of our own and make right what is wrong in this world."

I have never heard him speak such words. These words would get him killed. These words would make living in this place impossible. I cannot speak. I can only think of the children I have seen through the window, the child we would create would end as those children—beaten and killed. Is he so disconnected, I think, that he believes what he has said? I look into his face and see that he is tired and ill. My hatred for him melts for a moment before I speak. "You are insane," I say. It is the most I have ever talked back to him. I prepare to be hit, or worse.

Instead he reaches for a bottle of schnapps and takes a large drink. "Perhaps I am. Drink with me."

We sit at the kitchen table and drink until the liquor runs from our numbed mouths and our eyes roll backward into blackness. Morning's light pierces the room as my half-conscious brain registers the feel of his strong arms lifting me and carrying me into his bed. The next thing I remember is the feel of his hot semen penetrating my Jewish womb.

As my belly swells, and he realizes that soon the camp will know of my state, he refuses to allow other Nazis into his house. One night I rise from the bed to find him passed out at the kitchen table, drunk, a gun in his hands. What will become of me if he kills himself, I wonder? I will be in the hands of even greater enemies than this. I remove the gun from the table and linger over it, knowing that one bullet is all it will take to relieve me of this madness. One bullet in my head, and this may be the only chance. The growing child inside my womb kicks and I release my finger from the loaded gun and hide it in the cabinet away from his drunken madness.

He awakens the next morning in a foul mood. He drinks his coffee and spits it into the sink in disgust. "What is this?" It is his sickly mouth that has spoiled the taste. "You are trying to poison me."

I drink a cup myself to show him that it is fine. He falls to his knees and kneels before my protruding belly, his hands reaching to stroke it. I loosen myself from his grip and walk away, unable to withstand the insanity of his acts.

Suddenly there is a knock on the door. I run to the bedroom and hide.

"Where is she?" I hear them say. A mumbling of voices, angry and accusing reaches my ears. "Let us see her."

"No," I hear him say. "She is ill."

The heavy boots pound on the wooden floor. The door to the bedroom flies open. The covers rip away from my body. I am dragged to standing. The expressions are cold and lifeless. My face is slapped. My wrists are grabbed. I hear his pleading voice. "No!" he screams.

They push him aside and I am dragged from the house onto the grounds of the concentration camp. A young Jewish boy jumps backward, out of our path. He stares at me in horror. I close my eyes to shut out his face.

My Nazi has followed us. "Give her something to kill the pain!" Then I hear him say, "Do not kill our baby! Do not kill our baby!" His screams become wails. I am dragged into a room—it looks like an operating room. The lights are bright. The table is cold. Instruments of torture shine from the cabinets.

"The child is a Jew. You are a Jew." It is the only explanation given me. Four men hold me down as I struggle in panic and terror. I hear myself screaming, but it sounds far away. I cannot see my Nazi. I can only hear his cries. He begs and begs. "No! No!"

I am laid on the table and strapped down. My Nazi is in the room but they do not listen to his cries to ease my suffering. It is my suffering they live for. It is only my suffering that makes them feel alive. The knives are drawn.

From my Nazi I hear the cries, "I love you! I love you! I love you. It is my child. It is my child. I claim my child. I love you my sweet Jew. I love you my sweet Jew. I love you..." fades into the crack of bone and bruising of flesh, repeating over and over as his cries are muffled and his body softens beneath their fists and boots.

My abdomen is cut and the fetus dragged from my womb as his cries are silenced and his body dies. Then all is silence. I too am dead. Suddenly with great freedom our hearts are joined. A chord rises from our chests and joins us in our shared death. I love you, the chord cries out. I forgive you, the chord cries out. God, help us. There is only silence as we rise into the land of Spirit....

The healing of Spirit begins as a dance. The Jewish girl I was stands before me. I remember all the things about her I loved. Her bravery, her compassion, her beautiful eyes and skin. I must retrieve those parts of her I love.

A sleek and wise Black Panther comes to me. *I will assist in your Journey of Healing*, I hear him say. My Jewish girl is ringed by panthers and leopards. They rise onto their hind legs and begin a slow dance, circling her and circling her. *Draw to yourself all those things you love about her*, I am directed by the Black Panther. The big cats dance faster and faster, lifting her into the air, drawing her into my heart.

In my mind's eye I see the Panther as he lies on my chest. His hot, sensual breath warms my face. He opens his large mouth and places it onto mine. *Breathe out your sorrow*, he instructs me. *I can take it. Breathe out your pain and anger*, he says. *I can take it*. I breathe into his warm, moist mouth my sorrows, and he swallows them into his Greatness and flies away into the sky. *Reclaim your power*, I hear him say as he flies away. *Reclaim your power by placing me in your heart. I am here to protect you. I am here to comfort you. I am your symbol of Divine Love. On the other side of Fear there is always Love. After all, Love is Eternal.*

Before dawn the next morning I am awoken by the sound of someone whistling in the hallway. The whistling grows louder as the person moves closer then stops outside my door. What's that tune? *There's No Business Like Show Business?*

My body, curled up and stiffened from a night on the floor, moves slowly. I wince from the pain in my hip as I rise to standing and throw on a bathrobe. The whistling continues.

I open the door a crack and see a man leaning on a mop handle that is stuck inside a rolling bucket of dirty water. "Morning," he says.

"Morning," I reply. "You're up early this morning."

"No earlier than you," he says.

"You are a hell of a lot cheerier than I am," I say.

"You're an actress so why don't you try and act happy? Then maybe you'll convince yourself."

"How did you know I was an actress?"

"We've met before."

"We have?"

He holds out a clean, white hanky. "Yep. You look pretty rough. Why don't you take my hanky and wipe the dark circles away from under your eyes."

I take it from him and wipe under my right eye. When I pull it away there is a large, black smudge. "Sorry," I say as I show it to him.

"No problem. Keep it. I've got a million of them."

I put the hanky to my other eye and wipe. "Smells good," I say and take a whiff of the fabric. "Like jasmine."

He smiles and indicates he wants to come into my room. I hesitate. "You need to clean?" I ask.

He steps by me and closes the door behind him. "Nope, not to clean. To talk."

"Talk? About what?" I'm nervous now, thinking perhaps he's another patient posing as a janitor.

"You."

"Me?"

"You and why you're here." He takes a seat on the only chair in the room.

"Why do you care if I'm here?" I ask.

"It's my business to care."

I scan the room for a nurses call button should I need one. "Your business to care?"

"You don't remember me?"

I shake my head.

"Can I ask you a question?"

"Sure."

"How many angels can dance on the head of a pin?"

I shake my head. "When I wake up, will you be a janitor again?"

"Okay, one more question, then I'll leave you alone—if you want."

"Shoot."

He smiles, his eyes peering deeply through my fog. "How many somersaults can an angel do in the park?"

I stare at him, snort. "Oh, right. If you are my angel then I'm glad because I'm really pissed off right now. I'm pissed at you and God."

"It's a start. You finally acknowledge the existence of something greater than yourself," he says.

"Listen. Religion has done nothing but cause trouble in my life. I have no use for it. Not Judaism, Christianity or Buddhism."

"Understandable. Then make up your own. You have Spirit, don't you? Or did you lose that too?"

"Spirit? You want to waltz into my life, spew some words of wisdom and then disappear again. What, you get paid by the number of visits?"

He laughs. "So you do remember me. Central Park and the performing arts camp."

I lift my eyebrows in surprise. "So you are my angel. But I really am pissed. How about you sticking around on the material plane for awhile and then we'll talk. It's easy for you, you can spread your wings or whatever it is you do and evaporate."

"It's a vibrational shift. I vibrate at a frequency you can't perceive."

"Whatever."

"What did I tell you that night long ago? The night we sat together on a log under a full moon?"

"I can't remember."

"That's not true. I heard you tell your therapist. You said, 'The hell-fire of life consumes only the best of men, the rest stand by warming their hands.' Welcome to the hell-fire, Victoria."

He leans forward, as impossible as it seems, there is even more intensity in his eyes. "A pea leaps to the edge of the pot where it's boiling. 'Why are you boiling me?' it asks. The chef knocks him back down with a spoon. 'Don't try to escape. You think I'm harming you but I'm giving you flavor so you can mix with other flavors and foods and become the beauty that is human. Remember when you drank the rain that fell into the garden? That was for this moment. Grace begins it, then sexual enhancement, then new life emerges as something good to eat.' Eventually the pea says to the cook, 'Cook me some more. Hit me with your ladle. I can't do it alone.'"

"I suppose Rumi stole that from you back in the thirteenth century," I say snidely.

He leans back on the chair and a cigarette materializes between his fingertips. "I always liked the metaphor." He reaches the cigarette out toward me, "I know you're dying for one," he says.

"Thanks." I lean over and take it, expecting to see a halo or a pair of wings for a logo. I chuckle. It's a Camel. I light it from his proffered match. "Seems a bit odd, my angel giving me a cigarette."

"You look like you could use it." He shrugs. "It's not my job to judge. Besides you'll probably give them up for good in a year."

"You can see into the future?"

"Future possibilities. Only possibilities; don't forget you have free will. You kicked your therapist in the stomach because you have free will."

"I thought I was in Dachau. Besides, he *probably* deserved it."

"You could have left him at any time. You knew he wasn't helping you to work through your past lives."

"Yeah, but who else would I have gone to?" I ask.

"For your information there is a therapist who does past life regression about thirty minutes from here. If you had tried you could have found her. But, no… your stubborn streak prevented you. Just like with the theater critic, John Perry, you assume something and don't bother to question your assumption. But that's free will and we have to let you take your own path even when it's the harder path to take." He smiles at me. "So really, you have no one to blame but yourself for being in here."

"Thanks, you've really cheered me up."

"I don't care about cheering you up. I care about bucking you up. Your art, the theater, that's your passion. It one of the ways you connect to Spirit best. You've got talent, Victoria, don't waste it."

I stub the cigarette out on the windowsill. "That's what Tom said."

"Angels come in many guises."

A knock on the door causes both of us to turn our heads. When I turn back around he is gone. "Just like Star Trek." A tinkling laugh shimmers in the air.

Dr. Maura Farrell enters the room. "How are you?" she asks.

Better until you arrived.

Chapter Thirty

After seventy-two hours in Towering Pines they let me out with a prescription for an anti-depressant that makes me feel like shit. Upon returning home the first thing I do is toss the prescription into the wastebasket and look for my sketchbook. Three of the images of my Jewish life are still strong and the sketches flow easily through my hands. One—the Nazi passed out with his head on the kitchen table and the gun in his hands. Two—the view from the kitchen window of the child's eyes staring up at me. Three—the Nazis dragging me across the concentration camp on the way to the operating room.

The doorbell rings. Reluctantly I lift myself up to standing and answer the door. It's Dennis.

He looks at me, then down at his shoes and then once again at me. I step aside and gesture with my hand that he is welcome to enter.

"How have you been?" he asks.

"I'm surviving. You?"

"Okay." He smiles faintly.

"Want some tea or coffee?" I ask.

"Sure. Coffee if you have it."

I walk into the kitchen and he follows me. He sits on the kitchen chair and I pull the beans out of the cabinet and grind them.

"I probably shouldn't have come today. You didn't answer my note and I should leave it alone. I have no right. There seems no way out of this." He clenches his teeth and his jaw tightens noticeably. "Damn it, Victoria. I just want some answers. Why do you pull on my heart so? Why do you tear me apart? Why can't I forget about you?"

I stare at his twisted face and shaking hands.

He lays his head on the kitchen table to hide his contorted, painful expression. "I love you, Victoria. Somewhere deep inside of me I love you and I don't understand why. Damn it! I want to resolve this." He lifts his face from the table. "I'm so sorry."

A chill rises the length of my spine and erupts from the top of my head; a cold fountain streams forth until it covers me and brings up a trembling I can't hope to control.

He holds out his arms to me and I walk slowly into them and kneel on the floor before him. "I think I understand," I whisper. "I think I understand why we feel this way."

"What is it?" he asks.

"Lifetimes," I say. "Lifetimes of pain. Lifetimes of love, both twisted and pure."

He leans over and kisses me on the mouth, slowly and tenderly. "Can we make it right?" he asks.

"I don't know," I answer honestly. I grab him and kiss him again and again. I don't want to talk about it. I just want to feel him.

"Tell me," he says.

I put my finger across his mouth to silence him. I take his hand and pull him from the chair and lead him to the living room. "There," I say and point to the sketches on the floor.

"What are they?" He kneels down and studies the charcoal drawings.

"Do you remember?"

"Remember?" he asks.

"We were there."

He sits cross-legged on the floor and lifts one of the sketches to his lap. "Where is this?" he asks.

"Dachau," I say.

He looks up at me. His eyes narrow. "Dachau? You're kidding?"

"No. I'm not."

He stares down at the pictures.

"Close your eyes," I say. "Close your eyes and imagine you have boots on your feet. Army boots. Imagine you are wearing a Nazi uniform." I see his hands shake. He drops the sketch to the floor. "Go on, close your eyes." I sit next to him and take his hand in mine. "Listen and remember."

Dennis does as he is told. He closes his eyes, but his hands are cold to the touch and tremble slightly.

"Remember a place too horrible to imagine. Remember a time too horrible to forget."

Suddenly Dennis shakes and trembles. "Something is going to happen. Something bad. My heart is pounding."

"Stay where you are. Breathe, relax," I say.

"I don't know if I can do this," Dennis says.

"Let's go to the first time you are in uniform," I say. "Can you remember it?"

Dennis is quiet for a long time. When he speaks once again his voice has changed. He sounds like an adolescent boy and I detect a slight German accent.

… Karl Beier was fifteen when Hitler came to power. The Germany he remembers as a young boy was devastated by economic inflation. Karl recalls the excitement the people felt when a man by the name of Adolf Hitler became chancellor. He saw Hitler speak for the first time at a Nazi party rally and was overwhelmed with emotion. All his friends felt the same. Soon it was required of him to join the Nazi Party. Everyone was exhausted and hungry from Germany's long history of trouble….

"Every man had to join. I joined—it was the law. We were going to restore Germany to greatness. We were so tired of starving to death. I was very proud. I rose quickly in the ranks. I was a good soldier. I did what I was told and didn't ask questions. The movement was incredibly powerful. I gained such strength in joining my life with these other men and with the goal to bring Germany to glory. It was an exciting time for me."

"Was there a time when it began to change for you?" I ask.

"Yes," Dennis whispers. His voice still contains a hint of a German accent.

"Do you remember a time when you went with some other Nazis to find a traitor who was leaving on an airplane?"

"When you said that I got a picture in my mind. I think I'm much older now, maybe in my twenties. Not so innocent. I see black cars parked on the runway. A propeller plane. Some men are walking out to the plane," Dennis says. He clutches his face in his hands. "I can't look at this."

"What's happening?" I ask.

"They kill somebody. I throw the body out onto the ground. We are going to kill everyone on the plane unless the man we want confesses. Wait! A woman confesses. It isn't her, she isn't the one we want, but I end up with her. I'm not sure why, it's very confusing. I know they are going to kill everyone and I want to leave. I decide to take the woman and get away from there."

"That woman is me in my last life."

"Oh my God, Victoria." Dennis begins to cry.

I have been hearing all this with a mixture of emotion. Now when it is my turn to join in the story I find all I need to do is to close my eyes and I am there again.

"I remember driving in the car with you. Do you remember that?" I ask.

"Yes," he answers.

"What were you thinking?"

"I was wondering if you were a Jew. I suspected you were. Part of me didn't want to know. I am wondering what to do with you, at the same time I was... planning," he says.

"I'm terrified," I say.

"I know," he says quietly. "I'm so sorry. I don't understand it, but I felt sorry for you. I wanted to save your life."

"Why?" I ask.

"Because... because... they..." Dennis begins. He curls up into a ball and weeps. "Because they would kill you."

Instinctively I curl my body into his, and cry into his back. Neither of us speaks for a long time. Then Dennis says, "I was so sickened by what was happening. I didn't... I didn't know what else to do. So much death and pain."

"Do you remember when you take me to your home?" I ask.

"Yes," he whispers. "I remember. I thought if I kept you to myself it would go better for you. I was emotionally dead anyway by that point. I don't know why I cared, but I did. I decided to care about you in my own sick way." He cries again and I hold him. "How can I forgive myself?" he says.

"Do you remember what happened to us? Do you remember when I get pregnant?"

Dennis is silent for a long time. His breathing increases. His body tenses. I hold him tightly and rock him in my arms. I feel the circle is complete. At last there is no bad guy and no good guy, no hate and bitterness—the Jew comforts the Nazi the Nazi comforts the Jew. Finally Dennis says, "I don't want them to take you. I can't save you."

I am trembling and terrified, the feelings returning in my body as he remembers the event. I begin to scream, "No! No!"

Dennis answers my cry, "No! No!" His body twitches and flails. "They are killing me. Punching me. Kicking me."

"Hold onto me," I say to Dennis. "Hold me."

We return to full consciousness slowly. When we look at each other now there is a loving kindness that had been missing prior to the session. There are no secrets anymore—no dark hallways, no dusty corners. Although weak and tired, the Light shines in our eyes.

I do not hate this man. As I realize this and I look at him all the connections become clear to me. I see how I rescued him when he was the boy trembling in fear against the stone wall, his mother lying dead at his feet; and how he rescued me when I was a Jew ready to be killed by Nazis. We have both been the Victim and the Perpetrator, the Captor and the Captive. The line between Sinner and Saint becomes blurred.

"It wasn't our moment of infinite darkness," I say. "It was our moment of infinite light. Our moment of pure hell was also our moment of pure redemption. I see it now."

He is quiet beside me.

"We are tied," I say. "Tied by many lifetimes. So much pain and anger. I want to heal it. I *have* to heal it."

"What do you know?" he says to me. "Tell me what you know."

I tell him of the Roman man I was and how I murdered him in a jealous rage. I tell him of the lovers found out by the jealous husband. I tell him how I think it relates to Franklin and Jean.

We are silent for a long time. Then Shakespeare's sonnet comes to my mind:

"When to the sessions of sweet silent thought," I begin.

"I summon up remembrance of things past," Dennis says.

"I sigh the lack of many a thing I sought," I continue. "And with old woes new wail my dear time's waste. Then can I drown an eye, unus'd to flow, For precious friends hid in death's dateless night, And weep afresh love's long since cancel'd woe, And moan th' expense of many a vanish'd sight. Then can I grieve at grievances foregone, And heavily from woe to woe tell o'er The sad account of fore-bemoaned moan, Which I new pay as if not paid before."

Dennis finishes the sonnet for me: "But if the while I think on thee, dear friend, All losses are restor'd, and sorrows end."

"Amen," I say.

"Amen," he replies.

Chapter Thirty-One

On Monday I carry the sketches of Dachau with me to Ted's office and lay them down on the coffee table in front of him.

"Let me start," I say.

He looks at the sketches for a minute then clears his throat. "You spent seventy-two hours in Towering Pines and you bring me sketches."

"Dachau. My life in Dachau."

He doesn't answer, but crosses his arms against his chest and stares at me. I gather the sketches into my arms.

"Then I guess this is goodbye," I say.

"Don't do this, Victoria."

I walk from the room and shut the door. Then I come back and stick my head inside. "Don't worry, Ted. You'll get paid for today."

I walk across the street to sit in the little park. It's a gathering place for retirees; they go there to talk, play checkers, read the paper and feed the birds. An empty bench beckons and I sit down. I can't believe what just happened. That's how it ends? Then a thought occurs to me. What if Ted is right? What if I am crazy? What if Dennis is crazy? I look down at the sketches in my lap. Damn! I put my face in my hands. It's too much. I can't do this alone.

"Victoria?" Gary's father, Herman, touches me on the shoulder.

"Herman?" He sits down next to me, without being asked.

"What are you doing here?"

"Sitting," I say.

"Ah." He looks at his hands. "You know Gary closed the café?"

"What! When?"

"Yesterday was the last day. He gave up. He couldn't stand being surrounded by McDonalds, Dunkin' Donuts and Starbucks. Besides, he was tired. Ready for a change. He's getting married, you know."

My mouth is open, I snap it shut. "Really?" I say trying to sound uninterested. "And who's the lucky girl?"

"Linda White. She's Jewish, you know."

"No, I didn't."

"I bet you think that makes me happy," he says.

"Doesn't it?"

Herman shrugs. "What's that in your lap?" He reaches over and touches the sketches. "You are so talented with that. May I see them?"

As I hand them over I realize the connection but it's too late. Herman is staring at the picture of the Jewish girl being dragged across the concentration camp to her death.

He doesn't move for a long time, then he turns to face me. His expression is angry. "Who told you of this? Who?"

"What do you mean?"

"I've never spoken of it. How did you find out?"

"Find out what?"

"I remember like it was yesterday. I've spoken to no one about it, but the memory is seared into my mind. When I was in Dachau I was young and still had some strength. The Nazis took advantage of this and often I was assigned tasks out-of-doors. On this day I was cleaning the compound. I remember all too well, a young woman being dragged from one of the houses. I don't know who she was but I think she must have been Jewish. A Nazi officer ran behind them. Both of them were screaming and crying. I remember his words, 'Give her something to kill the pain. Do not—' "

"Kill our baby!" I say.

"Do not kill our baby," we say simultaneously.

Herman stares at me. I stare at Herman.

"You were there?" I ask.

"What do you mean? Of course, I was there. How do you know of this?" he says.

"Herman, I was there. I was that woman. The one they dragged across the ground."

"How can this... be?"

"Last lifetime. I am reincarnated from her. She is me. I am her. We are one."

"You are her? You are reincarnated from her? You, a non-Jew are her?" He points to the woman in the picture.

"Yes. They dragged me into the operating room and cut me open. They killed me and the baby."

"Oh, my God. That is so. That is what happened to her. The screams and cries filled the camp," he says.

"Herman, I was a Jew in Dachau, just like you were."

"Oh, my dear God." Herman throws his arms around me, lays his head on my chest and weeps. His tears fall onto the charcoal sketch. I watch them turn the sharp lines into soft edges and finally blend the image into one dark blot.

When Herman has finished crying I give him a hug and stand up from the bench. There is nothing more we can say. He must feel as confused as I did when Jean first appeared that day in the lecture hall. "It's true," I whisper and take my leave. When I am about twenty feet from him I turn around; he is staring at me, his eyes red, his face still carrying the look of disbelief. I wave goodbye and head over to Main Street to stand in front of the Café Bacchanal.

A *Closed Forever* sign is hung on the door, but when I press my nose to the glass everything looks exactly the same as it used to. On the far wall I see the sketches of my Victorian life. The smell of strong coffee and fresh baked goods still permeates the air outside. In my mind Gary has always been surrounded by the homey smell of bread—rich and yeasty.

That smell, why is it so familiar? I place my hand on the doorknob but I see a massive, rough hand slowly open the door to a small cottage. My large boots perform a clumsy tiptoe across the threshold. The wooden table—the woman, her hair swept up off her face. The smell of fresh baked bread. The baker, gone to market. Oh my God! It was Gary. The baker/husband was Gary. He walked in on me making love to his wife and tried to kill me! I walked in on him making love to Linda in this lifetime! Like a steel knife the revelation cuts into my consciousness.

Karma. But I didn't want to kill him. Not really. I still don't want to kill him. It has been softened. Karma has returned, but I've chosen not to seek revenge. I have free will. I can walk away and forgive him.

I turn from the café and head toward campus.

I knock on George's door, glad to see he is still working.

"Victoria. Have a seat. I'm just grading the last few final exams. By the way, I forgive you for your Hitler reference," he says, spreading his hands. "Mussolini, maybe. But Adolf?"

"Thanks." I smile, a truly happy smile. He responds with a look of relief. "By the way, George. I quit."

He puts down his pen and lifts his gaze. "You quit? Quit what?"

"Quit this. Teaching here. This job."

"You can't just quit. You've got tenure."

"Then I *un-tenure* myself."

"That's unheard of."

"Not anymore."

"Are you crazy?" he asks.

"My therapist seems to think so. I, however, think I'm finally getting sane. I'm going to Boston to work with Tom. He's asked me to be the Artistic Director for a repertory company there."

"So, take a temporary leave."

"Nope. Give my job to some hungry professor type. I need to quit." I stand to exit.

"So, we don't get any notice. Just, I quit. You'll never work in academia again."

"George, there are so many people dying for a job like this. You won't have trouble filling it. I don't care if I never work in academia. I'm done. It's history. It's all history."

I look around the office at the file cabinets piled high with books and papers. How many times have I stood in here? Apprehensive before my tenure, more confidently afterwards. How many times have I walked the paths and picked out the nervous Freshmen on the first day of school? Stood before a class and taken a deep breath before diving into a new term? Watched the sunlight hit these buildings on its way below the horizon, or the streetlights along the tree-lined pathways come on? Soon it would be gone.

Just like Victorian England, like Dachau, like the Roman baths or the life of a sea captain. Another memory, no more or less than that.

"How would you like it if I just up and left you in the lurch?" he asks.

"I have no doubt you'll get your chance. Next lifetime." I smile sweetly and shut the door on my way out.

978-0-595-34740-7
0-595-34740-1

Breinigsville, PA USA
04 March 2010

233570BV00001B/40/A